"Olivia! Blessed be the Lord."

"I had nowhere else to go. Don't send me out."

He inhaled a deep breath, wanting to sweep the forlorn figure into his arms and hold her close. "Of course I won't send you out. But you can't stay in here. It's too cold."

"Just find me another blanket, and I will be fine. I have been in worse situations."

"You don't know how worried I was. I searched everywhere for you."

"How did you find me?"

"I heard about the situation from Sally. It was Bodie who asked that you leave the house. He was worried. I told him there was no reason, but he did what he felt he must. I'm truly sorry."

Olivia shook her head. "I don't know what to do or where to go. I have not heard from my uncle. I'm a stranger in a hostile land, accused by everyone and wanted by no one."

"That isn't true." He came inside and sat down beside her. "You're wanted by me. More than you know."

LAURALEE BLISS

is a published author of over twenty romance novels and novellas. Lauralee enjoys writing books that are reminiscent of a roller-coaster ride for the reader. Her desire is that readers will come away with both an entertaining story and a lesson that ministers to the heart. She and her family have spent many happy summers on the Outer Banks of North Carolina where this series is set. It is a distinct honor to bring to life the history of the area, including the heroic deeds of the lifesaving stations' surfmen, who saved many from the dangerous seas. Lauralee makes her home in Virginia in the foothills of the Blue Ridge Mountains with her husband, Steve, and dogs Katie and Eve.

Website: www.lauraleebliss.com

Facebook: www.facebook.com/pages/
Readers-of-Author-Lauralee-Bliss

Twitter: @LauraleeBliss

LAURALEE BLISS

The Lady's Rescuer

HEARTSONG
PRESENTS

Recycling programs for this product may not exist in your area.

ISBN-13: 978-0-373-48764-6

The Lady's Rescuer

This edition published by arrangement with Love Inspired Books.

www.Harlequin.com

Printed in U.S.A.

God is our refuge and strength,
a very present help in trouble.
—*Psalms* 46:1

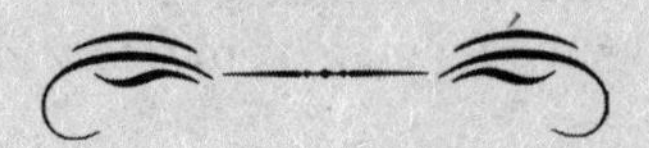

For my dear Aunt Charlotte, a true artist
who wholeheartedly supported my writing. I love you.

To Kathy for helping bring this series to life in print,
and to my agent, Tamela,
for never giving up on my story ideas.

Chapter 1

Hatteras Island, North Carolina
1881

"It shouldn't be long now, lass. We tack down the coast for another day or so. By late tomorrow we ought to be in Wilmington for sure."

"But that will put us to port at night, will it not?" Olivia Madison looked up at the burly sailor, her heart filled with dismay. She disliked arriving in the dead of night when darkness appeared ready to swallow ships and their unsuspecting crews. She also hated it for other reasons. Darkness had come when her parents succumbed to disease—her mother when she was a little girl and her father to a strange fever just a year ago. Then darkness had taken her only living family member, her twin brother, Nathan, arrested in the dead of night with no one there to help him. Darkness and light were not alike to her, despite what Scripture said.

Olivia refused to let her fellow sailors know her fear of darkness. Instead she stood tall like the main mast and tightened the belt that held up pants far too large for her slight frame. Olivia gripped a mast with one hand while shielding her eyes from the glare of the sun with the other. It had been a long journey, but she felt the end was near. The other crew members on board the schooner had performed their duties admirably, safeguarding passage across the vast ocean. Father had chosen his men well.

Tears sprang in her eyes when she thought of him. Broad-shouldered, able-bodied, but with a twinkle in his blue eyes, strength permeated his very being both as a ship's captain and as her father. Sadly he'd lacked the strength to overcome the fever that had claimed his life.

What had followed both amazed Olivia and helped ease her grief. The sailors who had worked for her father all left their ports of call to attend the funeral. Each of them pledged their devotion if ever she needed it. Now was that time, with Nathan's life at stake. Her brother had been imprisoned wrongly. And Olivia was taking this journey to help set him free.

"You're certainly quiet," commented a sailor named O'Malley. An Irish sailor on an English vessel seemed a great irony, but it was all Father's doing. He was no respecter of persons. He had always treated the Irish, the Scots and the English as if they were brothers. Father had united the men. No wonder the sailors loved him so.

More tears glazed her eyes, and she deftly wiped them away. "I only pray we will accomplish what we set out to do," she answered the man.

"We will, never fear. You have your father in you. You won't rest until this mission is done, and soon it will be." He patted her on the shoulder as a father would his daughter.

Several of her father's loyal sailors, including O'Malley, had answered her call for help in this venture. And so had others. In the crates concealed in the ship's bowels were family jewels and heirlooms, along with possessions given by wealthy friends, ready to pay off the rogue who'd imprisoned her dear brother. She tensed at the mere thought of the man who'd betrayed Nathan in a poor business deal. He had taken all the money, leaving Nathan with debts he could not pay. Now the dreadful debtor's prison was his lot, but not for much longer. Not if Olivia had anything to do with it.

She shook herself from her thoughts and considered the man before her, one of her father's favorites. "Are you still eager to see America, O'Malley?" she asked.

He grinned. "Of course! Not a sailor among us doesn't wish they could live there. The weeks we'll spend in Wilmington while you are visiting your uncle in Raleigh will be like a holiday to us."

Olivia wished she could share in the excitement. Instead a certain anxiety prevailed. America was a land she knew so little about. She'd heard many speak about it. It didn't seem so very different from England, though ports on this side of the Atlantic were few and far between. Now they sailed south along the Carolina coast of an endless sandy shore, nearing their goal and the completion of a long journey. They'd had but one storm to contend with, and even that wasn't so terrible.

Soon she would meet for the first time her only living relative besides her brother—her uncle, Dwight Browning. Dwight Browning was a prominent figure in the city of Raleigh, with many powerful people in his circle of friends. Informing him of Nathan's pitiful and increasingly sickly state, he'd urged her to come to America with the possessions she was able to gain through close friends and the wealth left in the estate. He would personally see to their sale and quickly raise the money needed to pay Nathan's debt.

I will do what needs to be done. Father would be proud if he were alive.

Olivia turned and headed below deck to the small cabin normally reserved for the captain. Inside the tiny room she knelt beside a large trunk and fumbled for the buckles. Resting atop the many belongings she carried from her native England lay her leather-bound journal, safely stored in oilskin in a box made of maple. She slowly slid back the top to the box and drew out the journal, eager to add another entry. Her heart fluttered. This time tomorrow her journal would boast of a triumphant landing at Wilmington, followed by her arrival in her uncle's company a week later. In a few months, God willing and with the work of her industrious uncle, she would revel in Nathan's freedom.

A knock came on the cabin door. Her maid, Alicia, opened it to find O'Malley with a grim look on his face. "The wind's changin', lass, and storm clouds are on the horizon. We may yet be delayed. So it 'tis with Providence in these things. We can only trust to His goodwill. Stay below deck."

Olivia quickly shut the trunk, even as Alicia stared with large eyes. The ship began to lurch. "Oh, miss, it's a storm!"

"It will be all right," she said as calmly as she could muster as the room swayed to and fro. Even now she doubted her own words. *Please, God, we are but a breath away. Please let us arrive in safety!*

Jacob Harris looked out over the ocean that churned with white-capped waves, the relentless salt water hungrily lapping the sandy beach. A misty fog rolled in with the waves. "I hope there's no ships out tonight, Jake. It looks like it could get rough," said Bodie, his fellow surfman in training.

Behind them, the glimmer of light from the lifesaving station's watchtower faded in the fog. Large raindrops splattered on them from thick clouds that hid the night stars. "We are definitely going to see a good storm," he agreed with his companion. "Come on. It's three miles to the substation. I'll show you what you need to do."

He felt in his pocket for the medal he would give to the surfmen of the next station, letting them know he and Bodie had done their part in the nightly beach patrol. But the brewing storm mirrored the personal storm within him. Earlier that day, he'd received the worst news possible. The lovely and fair Rose Leighton, his lifelong friend and love, returned to him the silver thimble he'd given to her as a promise of marriage many months ago. Jake still winced when he remembered her words. "I will not be your wife, Jacob," she had declared.

Even now Jake could feel the small lump of the precious object in his breast pocket, beneath the heavy, oiled canvas coat he wore while on patrol. "Why?" he had pleaded with her. "I do not understand." He felt like a sailor in one of the shipwrecks, watching a rope slipping quickly out of his sweaty palms, sending him into the frothing ocean below.

"I can't bear the thought of you going out into the storm to save others," she had said. "You believe you are braving the seas, but you don't care that you could be hurt—or even drown." Her voice faded away. "I won't live with that kind of fear, thinking I could lose you."

He took some measure of comfort knowing that she cared whether he lived or died. Being the surfman of a lifesaving station was dangerous, to be sure. But he had saved countless lives and cargoes without incident. Wasn't that worth some sacrifice? "Rose, please understand. My calling is to save others from drowning. I may sometimes need to risk my life, but others will die if I don't."

Rose had trembled at his words. "If the wind and storms can sink boats and kill people, think what it could do to you! And me. I could be a widow." She shook her head and turned away. "I'm sorry."

Jake shook himself out of his reverie, shuddering from the memory of Rose's words. Bodie cast him a curious glance as they swung their lanterns. They turned their gazes outward to the ocean, looking for any ships in distress.

"What's wrong?" Bodie finally asked. "You don't seem yourself."

Jake did not want to tell him what had happened with Rose and the embarrassment he felt. Yet he could not quell his friend's curiosity. He quickly explained the broken proposal.

"I'm sorry to hear that. I liked Rose."

"It doesn't matter," he said, searching for the words to lift his confidence. "I'm married to the sea anyway. It's the life I have chosen."

"Not me," Bodie said. "I'm not marrying no sea. I mean, I like this work so far, but I love Sally too much."

"Does she like that you're a surfman?"

"Of course. She thinks it's grand. She calls me her hero. She even likes the fact that I share the same name with the lighthouse up the coast there."

Jake winced. How he wished Rose had felt the same way. He paused to scan the distant horizon, and suddenly he saw something. A blink of a white light through the rolling fog. His fingers tensed around the handle of the lantern, which he raised higher in the darkness. All thoughts of Rose vanished at this telltale sign.

Bodie stood beside him, also scanning the ocean. "What's the matter? Do you see something?"

"I thought I saw a light flash. Can you make out anything?"

"Not really. It's too foggy."

Jake continued to stare. "There it is again! See that? It could be a passing ship or it could be one in distress. Take my lantern and hold them both high. The brightness will let them know where the shoreline is. I hope they saw your lighthouse up north warning them of the coastline."

Bodie's hands trembled as he held the lanterns high. "There it is again!" Jake exclaimed. "It's not far from the coast. I'll shoot off a signal, then we need to get back to the station and alert the others." He lit the Coston signal or flare he carried in a pouch while excitement and nervousness bubbled up inside him. "We need to inform the keeper." He began running back toward the station with Bodie right behind him. "I'm sure they saw it from the watchtower."

Bodie said nothing as he followed. When Jake saw the other surfmen readying the equipment, his fear was confirmed. He inhaled a sharp breath to calm his rapidly beating heart.

"We saw the signal, and the keeper gave the order," shouted Grayson Long, surfman number one. "The ship is lodged on the sand bar. It's close enough to use the beach apparatus. As it is, the seas are growing rough."

When another signal, white in color, pierced the bank of clouds hovering over the ocean, Jake knew that tonight they were called upon to save lives. Raindrops pelted him in the face, sending water dripping into his eyes. He brushed it away, thinking of the verse from a well-known hymn while the men worked to ready the equipment that would aid the ship:

Trim your feeble lamp, my brother
Some poor sailor tempest tos't
Trying now to make the harbor,
In the darkness may be lost.
Let the lower lights be burning,
Send a gleam across the wave,
Some poor fainting, struggling seaman,
You may rescue, you may save.

A chill of anxiety coursed through him for an instant before being replaced by determination. *Lord, I know now I could never ignore a life that might be saved in exchange for a hand in marriage. Even if it's the woman I love.* His fingers slipped on the wet ropes as men yelled at each other, ready to shoot the line from the cannon out to the imperiled ship. *This is what I'm called to do. This is all that matters. Lord, You saved others from death when You gave Your life. Can I do any less?* The thoughts strengthened his resolve to do what mattered most. The troubled ship and its crew had made the decision for him.

Jake jumped when the Lyle gun fired, hurling shot and a line toward the distressed ship. He prayed the sailors there would know how to rig it so they could then feed the breeches buoy out to them. When the line turned taut, he sighed in relief.

Grayson slapped Jake on the shoulder. "They are ready for us to save them," he said.

The keeper signaled for him. "Jake, I want you to go out first," he said, pointing to the breeches buoy made of heavy fabric with strong lines that would feed him to the ship. Jake wasted no time doing as the leader asked. He wiped rainwater from his face as the storm beat down even harder and climbed into the breeches assembly. He soon felt himself being pulled out into the raging ocean waters. His feet caught in the waves. Water poured into his boots, pulling him downward against the fabric of the apparatus. He held on and squinted as he slowly approached the disabled schooner, caught on a rough sandbar that had likely torn a hole in the hull. Debris floated in the ocean as the ship listed to one side. His heart began to race. Little time remained before the vessel sank.

Jake climbed on board to find a burly man pacing on the slanted deck, muttering words, an anxious look on his face. He quickly poured the water out of his boots.

"Help us, man," said the burly sailor, his hand reaching out to Jake. "She won't wake up."

Jake looked around. "Where is the rest of the crew?"

The man shook his head. "We are all that's left."

Jake winced but couldn't dwell on the sorrowful news of lives lost. Right now he had two lives to save. His gaze now fell on a woman lying prostrate on the ship's deck. "We don't have much time," he told the sailor. "Your vessel is taking on water. Help me get her into the breeches assembly. I will get it in first, then you will help position her in front."

The man complied with Jake giving instructions, feeding her legs between the ropes in front of him. Jake gripped her firmly for safety and gave the signal. He murmured a prayer for the ropes to hold fast and the men onshore to work quickly to bring them in. *Help us, God, before it's too late!*

Chapter 2

Olivia fought against the trap, trying to scream. How she wanted out of this terrible thing that nearly strangled her! To ask who it was that gripped her hard with hands burrowing into her flesh and why she seemed tangled in ropes! A voice in her ear told her everything would be all right. She must stay calm. *Don't be afraid,* she thought. *Say a prayer. It's all you can do.*

She'd heard the same words about prayer from the first mate O'Malley, before the ship's bell sounded. A huge wave had crashed over the small vessel, sending it against a sandbar with a terrible crack. Shouts of panic followed with screams as the ship tilted. Bodies flew into the frigid waters. *Was it all a dream?* she wondered. *Did it really happen?*

Again she tried to rid herself of the firm hands that held her, and again a strange but soothing voice above the tumult tried to reassure her that everything would be all right. How could any of those words be true? She struggled and managed to look down with one eye to see an oily darkness with a glimmer on the surface. Her feet were dragging through water. Straining to look behind, some man was holding her in the strangest contraption she'd ever seen. The device that bore her bounced up and down along ropes that pulled it to shore. *This is a terrible dream. This cannot be happening to me!*

When at last they arrived on land, she heard the voices of men all around her. She could do little except allow them to take her out of the dreadful contraption that had dragged her through the cold water, away from the ship and its precious cargo. A device, dreadful though it may have been, that might have saved her life. She tried to focus on the images around her, but her vision was blurred from seawater.

"My ship," she managed to croak. "O'Malley? Where are you? Please."

"Grayson has gone to get him," she heard someone say.

Oh, thank You, God. He is alive. She struggled to sit up. When she did, she saw the contraption now bearing her first mate. O'Malley appeared bedraggled and worn. Strands of red hair clung to his face, and his beard dripped water. "What happened?" she asked her grizzly first mate.

"A-a bad storm, lass," he sputtered. "I thought… I thought we could outrun it by turning the ship. We couldn't. The ship is lost. Harlan, Braxton, Johnson are…"

"No!" She shut her eyes, overcome with sadness. What O'Malley said couldn't be true. She struggled to keep the tears at bay, even as the men helped her lie on a litter and covered her shivering form with blankets. They picked her up and carried her she knew not where. The litter bumped suddenly, nearly sending her to the sands below.

"Careful, Jake!" a stout voice admonished the man who carried the head of the litter.

"Jake's worn-out," said another. "Someone else should take the lead."

"I'm fine," the man named Jake answered.

But I'm not! Olivia pleaded. *Can't anyone hear me? I've lost the crew. The ship. The valuables, the precious cargo. What will I do?* How she wanted to shout it out loud, but she was too weak. Instead she looked around and again saw O'Malley. He walked hunched over, barely staggering through the wet sand. The burly Irishman prided himself on his skills at sea. No doubt he blamed himself for what had happened. She didn't want him burdened, but she could do little to ease it in her present state.

"We can't keep her here at the station," said another man with authority. "She should be taken to Mrs. Wilson's in the village."

"Mrs. Wilson is over on the mainland caring for her daughter who just had a baby, Grayson."

Olivia considered this. A woman alone with all these men was unseemly. But there was Alicia, her maid. "Alicia," she croaked. She again looked to O'Malley but he had turned away. "Alicia?"

"She calls for her maid," the burly O'Malley told the rescuer named Jake.

"She is too ill to be told."

Told what? Cold swept over her. *Not Alicia, too. No!* Losing the ship and the cargo was bad enough, but to have the sweet young girl sacrificed to the storm…it was too much to bear. Tears filled her eyes at the thought of the young woman and her caring ways. Finally she managed to say it. "No!"

The men all looked down at her.

She found the strength to sit up. "Alicia. The… the ship."

"I'm sorry," said the man they called Jake.

They carried her to a building and then to a warm bed. A new blanket was heaped on her but still her teeth chattered. Great heaves filled her throat. *Alicia. The ship. Nathan's only means of freedom. All gone.* How could God have allowed this? She tried to get up from the bed. She must do something, anything, or all would be lost.

A firm hand gently pushed her back. "You need to rest."

She blinked her eyes rapidly. They still burned from the caustic seawater. With her hand she flicked back wet, limp hair from her face. "Where is O'Malley? I—I must know everything. I am responsible for the ship."

A cup of something warm was given to her instead. As she sipped it, a great urgency rose up. For food, maybe. But more for knowledge. If only someone could send word to her uncle. Uncle Dwight would take command of this situation and tell her what to do.

"We can't care for a woman here at the station," Grayson Long said. "You know that, Jake."

Jake pretended not to hear as he fetched another blanket. All the women he knew—his mother, his sister, Rose—manned the home and hearth and had never commanded a ship. None were like this rescued passenger, or looked like her, dressed as if she were a part of the crew. But none of that mattered. She needed help, and he would provide it.

He laid another blanket over her still form, thankful she had drifted off to sleep after managing to drink down the warm broth.

"Jake?" Grayson said again.

"I know." He tried to think, but the events of the night left him exhausted. He saw Bodie venture in. "Bodie, would your Sally be able to help? It would be better if another woman could look after her. She and her mother have had boarders before."

"Sally's not really the nursing kind, but her mother might be. She's nursed folks." Bodie poured himself steaming coffee from the pot sitting on the cookstove. He drank some, then set down the cup, grabbed a biscuit and the first coat he could find that was still dry. "I'll go ask her."

"It's late, Bodie. It can wait until morning," Grayson said. "We've just got done with a rescue, and you're cold and wet."

"I'm fine." Bodie quickly donned the coat and slipped out into the rain-soaked darkness. Grayson shook his head and chuckled. Jake did as well, knowing Bodie would take any opportunity to see his love.

The mumblings of the man named O'Malley brought Jake back to reality. "What are we going to do?" the Irishman moaned. "'Tis my fault alone. The ship, the crew. All my fault."

"Sir, it's no one's fault," Jake began. "Have something to drink and eat."

O'Malley shook his head, refusing the coffee and food. Instead he wandered away down the coast, muttering about the ship, the crew and the cargo.

Despite his own weariness, Jake took a coat and hurried to follow the dazed Irishman, who was moving quickly in the darkness. "O'Malley!" he shouted, hoping to be heard over the roar of wind and waves. But soon the figure had vanished in the pelting raindrops. Jake inhaled a sharp breath and continued to call for the man.

Jake finally turned toward the glimmer of light in the windows of the lifesaving station. He could only hope the man would return soon. He couldn't bear to think what would happen if the woman learned yet another soul had been lost and she was the lone survivor.

Jake met Bodie outside the door to the station, breathless from his errand to see his beloved's family. "Sally's mother said the passenger can stay with them until she recovers. We will take her over in the morning. It's too late to do it now, of course."

"That's kind of them."

Bodie brushed back locks of wet hair and gazed around. "What are you doing out here anyway, Jake?"

"The big Irishman we rescued ran off. I think he blames himself for the ship's peril. I—I can't find him anywhere. I fear he may have..." He could not bring himself to voice his fear.

"He'll be back."

"I'm not so sure."

Once back in the station, Jake couldn't forget the Irishman taking off into the eye of the storm or the young woman he held close inside the breeches buoy. He peeked in the back room to find his charge still asleep. He returned and found a place at the table where the rest of the weary surfmen had assembled, bowls and spoons ready and eager to consume the hearty stew.

"So where's the rest of the ship's crew?" Richard inquired, having been elected to stay behind at the station during the rescue. "I only saw two come in."

Grayson shook his head while exchanging sorrowful looks with Jake.

"The woman and the big Irishman are all we found," Jake confirmed. "But now he's gone missing. He was mumbling something about the loss of the ship and crew and then disappeared."

Richard whistled before taking a huge bite of stew. The rest of the men sat somberly in their places, absorbing the news. Their duty, after all, was to save lives. They felt a measure of failure after hearing of souls lost.

"The storm blew up, quickly and deadly," Jake added. "I believe the keeper will agree that we did all we could. By the time I arrived at the vessel, only two of the crew were alive on deck."

"But to have them all lost," one mourned.

"It was a small craft. A schooner that only required a small crew. The storm must have taken them by surprise, as it does many of the ships in this region."

"Even with my lighthouse to warn them," Bodie added for effect as he ate his stew.

"Jake, do you have something else to share?" Grayson asked as if he could sense what was churning in his mind.

"I was thinking about the lighthouses. How they warn sailors of the dangerous coast. We also need to heed the warnings that come our way in life." He took a piece of bread. "I know sometimes I haven't. Any one of us could end up like the crew of this vessel, with no life or purpose in us."

The men ceased eating to stare at him.

Just then they heard a moan come from the back

room. Jake left the table and ventured in. He found the woman wide-awake, clutching the blankets, a look of terror contorting her face. "Save me!" she cried.

Without even thinking Jake came to her bedside and enfolded her gently in his arms. "It's all right now. You're safe."

But the wide-eyed look on her face spoke otherwise. The horror of the night had captured both her heart and soul. He felt helpless to take it away.

Chapter 3

Bright morning sunlight pierced through the window to the opposite wall. Olivia blinked open her eyes, confused. The ship no longer swayed as if dancing on the open waters. The furnishings were unfamiliar. This was not the tiny cabin aboard the schooner that had carried her from England to America.

She tossed aside the covers and swung her legs over the edge of the bed. Her feet touched a cold wooden floor below. The large window greeting her was not a port-size window. It was clear: she was no longer on board the ship.

Suddenly, fateful scenes came crashing down as fierce as the storm that had ripped apart the ship. The angry waves sending water over the deck. The wind whistling. O'Malley shouting commands in his thick Irish brogue, urging the sailors to quickly lower the sails. Then the terrible sound of splintering wood mixed with the cries of the fallen.

We shipwrecked! A shudder raced through her. She glanced down to see a simple nightgown. She barely remembered putting it on, urged by some female voice she thought was her maid, Alicia. Someone had been kind enough to take her in.

"Are you all right, miss?" came a tentative voice.

Olivia found a dressing gown and quickly slipped it on, pushing back a mound of her long thick hair still tainted with salt from the ocean. "I think so."

The door opened to reveal a woman she did not recognize. "Where…where am I?" Olivia asked.

"Oh, you're at my mother's house here in Hatteras Village. I'm Sally Hamilton."

"Thank you for taking me in. And I know my maid is…"

The young woman shook her head. "I'm sorry for your loss." Her eyes widened before the words spilled forth in rapid succession. "I've heard other stories too, that you were the captain of the vessel that shipwrecked last night off the coast. And when you came here, you were wearing men's trousers of all things. Why, I've never worn trousers in my life. Mother would have a fit and so would my friends. I've never heard of a woman captain, either."

Olivia frowned. *Oh no, a young girl with an incessant need to know everything.* She sighed. Still, she owed Sally and her mother a debt of gratitude. They cared, after all. They invited her here to recuperate. She prayed for patience. "I didn't captain the ship, but I did hire the men who brought me here from England. We came here to…" She paused, wondering how much she should divulge about her brother, Nathan, his circumstances and why she had come to America. "I came to America on business," she finally said. "Now everything is gone."

"I'm sorry for your loss," she said again. "My suitor, Henry, told me what happened to your ship and crew. He was with the men who saved you."

Olivia blinked, realizing then she had little memory of last evening's events or what happened except for the dreadful storm that consumed them. "I— I'm not sure what you mean."

"How your boat is gone and all the crew died. It's so sad."

Olivia grew rigid. She shook from a burst of cold dread. "No," she said softly. She hiccupped and managed a sordid chuckle. "They couldn't all have died! It couldn't have happened. I remember O'Malley and…"

"Henry told me one man survived, but he disappeared into the storm and no one knows where he went. They say for now you're the only survivor."

The only survivor. Olivia shook as the words rang like a solemn bell announcing some funeral procession. The faithful crew. Dear O'Malley. Her sweet little maid, Alicia, who Sally resembled in many ways.

All of them…gone. The pleasant sunshine streaming through the window now blinded her with its glare. Or was it the sting of tears in her eyes that blurred her vision? She began to heave.

"I—I will leave you alone. If you need anything, please let me know." Sally softly closed the door.

Tears instantly bubbled up in her eyes, ready to spill out. Olivia wiped them away as she had so often when sorrow tried to overwhelm her. Now was not the time to be sad but the time to act. *Now what do I do? I must try to find out about the cargo, to see if anything is left. It can't let it be lost too or all this would have been in vain. All those brave sailors will have perished for nothing and Nathan could die too. I must find out. And I must contact Uncle Dwight and tell him where I am.*

She forced away her sorrow and looked around for clothing to wear. If the ship was gone as the girl had said, so too was her trunk and trousseau. She owned nothing but the clothes she'd been wearing when the ship went down. She did not even have the blessed journal where she had painstakingly recorded her thoughts during the long journey across the Atlantic. The gravity of all this was more than she could bear. Loss seemed her continued lot in life. First the loss of her mother. Then her proud seafaring father. Her brother ensnared by a deceitful man. Her livelihood in England, including the fine manor home and all their holdings, all sold. Now the ship that carried the only means left to save the last of her family, and maybe her own peace, might well lie at the bottom of the Atlantic.

But she had not endured so much, even a voyage across the Atlantic, to be stopped here, wherever here was. She must find a way to salvage from the shipwreck the precious cargo. She would alert Uncle Dwight to come fetch her and the merchandise from this place. She would go on with his suggestion to sell what they had and then return in haste to England to pay the debt and save her brother. She refused to let any further catastrophe be her lot, as God was her witness.

Olivia hastened for the door and peered out. She heard the voices of a man and Sally conversing in a nearby room.

"Yes, she finally woke up, Henry. But I don't think she remembers what happened."

"Guess it's better she doesn't. I mean, she doesn't have anything or anyone. She's all alone."

"I know. I said something about that, and I think I upset her."

"A few things from the boat did wash ashore not far from the station. When she feels better, I'll show them to her."

"I think some good news like that would be better than any tonic."

Olivia heard nothing further and presumed the man was offering his lady an embrace of comfort. How she wouldn't mind arms around her right now, imparting comfort and reassurance. She recalled some vague embrace last evening from the man who had rescued her. But really, it was true: she had no one. Even Almighty God appeared absent from her situation. She was truly alone in a strange land. But at least she did hear that sundries had washed ashore. Perhaps hope still remained.

"Pardon me," Olivia now called out into the hallway. Sally and Henry came out of the sitting room and stood in the hall. The man appeared windblown with his bushy brown hair in disarray and his shirt untucked. "I'm sorry to bother you but I have need of something decent to wear?"

"Oh dear, you'd better go back to the station, Henry," Sally said, giving him a slight push along with a girlish giggle.

"I will. I'm glad you're better, miss," he added to Olivia. "Sally calls me Henry, but at the station everyone calls me Bodie. I'm named after the lighthouse up on Pea Island."

"I'm glad you are here." She gazed at length. "Did I hear you say that you found some remains from my ship?"

"Why yes, ma'am. Some of it has washed ashore. A few pieces of furniture and a box."

"What kind of box?"

"Oh, about so big." He spanned the dimensions with his hands. "It looks a little like an old portable writing desk. I think there's something in it. If the keeper lets me, I'll bring it by tonight if you want."

"Why don't you come for dinner?" Sally suggested with a coy smile. "You can tell Miss Madison here all about the rescue and the box you found. And we can spend a little more time together."

"I wasn't the one who rescued her. Jake did." Bodie looked at Olivia. "He's been asking about you, too. That's another reason I came by, to see how you're doing so I can report back to him."

"Maybe you should have this Jake come, too?" Olivia wondered, looking to Sally for approval.

"A wonderful idea. Can you see if he's free, Henry?"

"Just so long as we don't have a rescue tonight. It looks like good weather for now. And I'll get someone else to do the beach patrol. I'm sure Jake would be happy to come."

"Henry, you don't have to go on patrol *every* night, do you?" Sally emphasized the point, accompanied by a set of pouting red lips. "We'll never get to spend a quiet evening together."

"I know, Sally, but I like doing it. That's how we found out your ship was in trouble," he added to Olivia. "Jake saw the signal from your ship. He knew something was wrong even before the keeper raised the alarm. That's why I like working with him. He knows everything."

Olivia managed a small smile and thanked him. After the door shut, Sally went to fetch her a dress to wear while Olivia pondered the conversation. *So this Jake is my rescuer. He is the one who pulled me to safety. The one who asks about me...and who seems to know everything. He sounds like just the man I need to find out about my cargo.*

"She asked me to come?" Jake could hardly believe it when Bodie told him the news. He was in the midst of washing the breakfast bowls when Bodie burst in, his face all smiles, promptly informing him of the dinner invitation that night.

"Yes, she did. I told her how you rescued her. She probably wants to thank you personally."

A whistle pierced the air, sending both Jake and Bodie whirling at the sound. They found the surfman named John with a wide grin on his beefy face. Jake knew better than to have a conversation like this near the main living quarters where listening ears were ready for any titillating news. Especially John, who enjoyed spreading rumors about the fellow surfmen.

"Trying to hook another gal already, huh, Jake? You ought to let things settle down a bit before you sink your line in the water again. Didn't make out too well with the last gal, so's I hear. She got away." John laughed heartily.

Jake gritted his teeth. "We pulled passengers to safety last night, as I recall. That's my concern, as it should be yours."

"The woman you saved is interested in that box that washed ashore at sunup," Bodie continued. "Has anyone looked inside it yet?"

"Not if it's personal effects," Jake said. "The keeper doesn't permit it."

"Well, I looked inside it," John announced. "It's just some leather book, like a journal. Looks like it was kept by your new lady of the sea, Jake."

Jake opened his mouth to issue a rebuke.

"Now, don't get so uppity," John interrupted. "I was told I could look. Didn't see too many interesting things in it. Wasn't even worth it."

"I can't believe the keeper allowed you to read it!" Jake exclaimed. He'd never known it to be protocol to rifle through the possessions of survivors unless special permission was given. Especially a diary belonging to one of the shipwrecked crew. "Maybe I'll just ask the keeper about it and…"

John strode forward and planted himself directly in front of Jake. His eyes glared from a red face. "I wouldn't do that if I were you," he hissed, "'less you plan on finding yourself in big trouble."

"Then I'd suggest you be honest," Jake countered, "and leave alone the personal possessions that wash ashore. Or you might also find *yourself* in big trouble."

John continued to stare long and hard as if in a dare before wheeling about and striding away. Bodie came to Jake's side and whistled a sigh. "You shouldn't get him riled like that, Jake. You know him. You'll be the next one he'll be telling tales about."

"I don't care. He lied about the keeper giving him permission, and he invaded personal property. In fact, I ought to tell the keeper about it right now."

Bodie stretched out his hand as his blue eyes

widened in concern. "Don't do it. It's not worth it. C'mon, let's finish washing these pots, and I'll tell you more about what happened this morning at Sally's with that shipwrecked lady passenger."

Bodie was right. There was a blessing in being a peacemaker as the Bible said, even if the pain of injustice filled Jake. Or was it rather a defensiveness that rose up on behalf of Olivia Madison?

"I put in a good word for you, Jake," Bodie said, hooking the large kettle used to cook the morning mush back on the wall. "I told Miss Madison that you knew everything about rescuing. You've been teaching me everything I need to know."

Jake smirked. "You're learning a good deal on your own, too, Bodie." But he couldn't help the pride that filled him with the knowledge that Olivia wished to see him.

"Remember how I rigged the beach apparatus for the first time? The whole thing ended up falling in the water. Everyone laughed. But you showed me what to do, where to place the ropes and how to tie the right knots."

"You're a quick learner, Bodie. It isn't easy being the youngest and newest member of the crew." *And he had wisdom even in his youth,* Jake considered, *when he cautioned me not to stir up things with John.*

When they had finished the morning cleanup, Jake wandered out to the storage area to find the lead surfman, Grayson Long, looking over a cord of rope. He considered the man's friendship, thinking how Grayson had offered counsel in matters of life. Jake recalled an old friend telling him how everyone needed a Paul and a Timothy in his life. A Paul to minister and a Timothy to teach. Grayson to him was a Paul; Bodie was Jake's Timothy. As Bodie looked up to Jake, Jake looked to Grayson.

"What is it, Jake?" Grayson now asked with his back turned, his gaze focused on the tasks at hand.

"Isn't there a rule allowing shipwrecked passengers their effects if they are washed ashore?"

Grayson glanced at him. "Of course."

"I mean, if an item such as a journal happened to wash ashore, are we allowed to read it?"

Grayson hefted the coil of rope over one shoulder. "Why? Did you look at the journal in that box that came from the shipwreck?"

"John did. He claimed the keeper gave him permission. I'm sure he was lying. I was going to talk to the keeper about it, but Bodie said it would be better not to stir things up. That doesn't seem right."

"No, it isn't right. John knows we're not allowed to go through personal property unless lives depend on it. But I'm sure he was also curious."

"Ha. A fine excuse."

"No, it's not. But sometimes, Jake, you have to decide if the battle is worth fighting. To me, this is not worth the aggravation and division it could bring within the station. Especially when we need to work together to save others."

Jake's muscles tightened, and he opened his mouth to respond.

"Yes, I know," Grayson continued. "You don't agree. But what is there to be gained? So John looked at it. I can ask him about it later if you want. But to go against a fellow surfman who might be the one holding the rope that anchors you in the breeches buoy may not be the wisest course of action. You need to decide if this is important enough to risk a break in the ranks."

Jake chewed on his lower lip. They did need each other to work in unison during a full-fledged rescue effort. They had to be a band of brothers that looked out for one another in order to save lives from stricken ships.

"Help me check this line, will you? I thought I saw some fraying the other night during the rescue operation, and I need to see if we ought to replace it. I have it in mind to check up north at the Kinakeet station to see if they have extra line to spare."

Jake slid off the crate and talked about his dinner invitation from Olivia Madison and Sally's family while he stretched out the length of rope across the sandy ground. "What do you think, Grayson?"

"Do you think you ought to be getting involved with another woman so soon?"

"I'm not becoming involved. She only wishes to thank me, I'm sure." He felt warmth tease his cheeks. Surely he didn't give the impression that Olivia Madison meant anything more to him than a rescued passenger.

"I only meant that you appeared quite protective of her the night she was brought in. Not that you were wrong. I suppose if I had been the one in the breeches buoy, I'd want to see my passenger in good hands."

"Yes. I'm not sure why you or anyone else is making anything out of this. But if you think it isn't a good idea to go, I'll give my regrets."

Grayson chuckled. "Jake, you're a decent fellow. You deserve a good home-cooked meal and a friendly thank-you after what you did. So have a good time and remember us unfortunate surfmen who must endure Richard's cooking tonight."

Jake laughed as together they examined the rope until he spied the frayed section. He considered what might have happened had that rope given way during the rescue…like the sheer terror of being tossed into the ocean. He thought then of his arms around Olivia in the breeches buoy and suddenly the rope breaking, sending them sinking into the cold water. Just then, the good humor of the pending evening disappeared under a cloud of dread.

Chapter 4

Olivia stared at her reflection. Sally had lent one of her gowns for dinner, but the hemline dragged on the floor, taking with it every bit of sand and dust until the white of the gown quickly turned a dingy gray. The sleeves hung down to her knuckles.

There must be something about the sea air and living near the ocean that made a girl grow tall and willowy. Olivia was just the opposite, petite, narrow, perhaps delicate to some. No matter. She'd remain seated during the evening and keep her elbows bent so the sleeves appeared shorter. The men were not likely to linger anyway, with the need to return to their duties at the lifesaving station—duties that had saved her life.

At that moment she gazed at her right hand to see

her father's signet ring still on her forefinger. At least she had not lost that precious item. She traced the pattern of leaves that reminded her of the fine ivy that grew about the manor home, and the emblem of a seafaring vessel in honor of Father's work in maritime. She swallowed hard when she thought of him. Dear Father. Captain of his vessel. Then she thought of the brave men who had worked closely with him, who loved him and who came to serve her because of him. Now the same ones had given their lives to safeguard her passage here.

Olivia tried to shake away the thought that she was the sole survivor of the ordeal, but the pain was a stone that lodged in her throat. Thankfully her father wasn't alive to hear what had happened to his men. He would have been devastated.

She heard assorted voices then and realized the guests must have arrived. Olivia threw some water on her blotchy face and dried her eyes. She glanced again at the trailing gown at her feet and prayed she wouldn't trip on it. She opened the door, heaving a sigh, and suddenly felt nervous. Why should she? She'd been around men for several months on the high seas—rough sailors with a language all their own. Why should she be nervous for a simple meal with those who had performed admirable deeds? Olivia steadied herself and walked out into the hall where she heard voices coming from the sitting room.

"Oh, and here is Miss Madison!" Sally said with

a smile. Two men stood. Olivia curtsied, trying not to stare too much at the man dressed in black trousers and a white shirt, with sandy-colored hair, the roughness of beard stubble, and a thin line of a moustache above the upper lip. So this was the one who had held her in his arms as they were carried in a strange harness made of heavy canvas, through tumultuous wind and wave, to the safety of the shore.

"You already met my beau, Henry Greer," Sally introduced. "I prefer Henry to his nickname, Bodie. It's so much more distinguished. And this is Jacob Harris. We know him as Jake."

The man offered a small bow. "You are looking well, Miss Madison."

Her heart pounded slightly. "I hear that thanks for my rescue goes to you, Mr. Harris." She moved carefully across the room, trying not to step on the hem of the dress.

"I was afraid you had taken in some seawater, but you appear to have recovered."

His smile made her heart flutter once again.

"We've had passengers nearly drown," Bodie interjected. "We have to slam their stomach with a fist to make them spit up the water."

"Oh, for goodness' sake, Henry, must you explain it with such vulgarity?" Sally said with a huff. "Terrible."

Her tone brought the young man nearly to his knees as he came and sat down on the settee beside Sally, looping his arm around her. "I'm sorry, turtle dove. I wasn't thinking. I just know when a passenger gets like that, you have to act quickly to help them breathe, or sometimes they will never breathe again."

Olivia drew in a deep breath and felt a sting of tears. She turned aside and then saw Jake look at her with concern.

Sally shook her head. "We should talk about cheerful things." She pecked Henry's cheek, and he returned the favor with a full kiss on her lips.

The romantic interlude made Olivia shift in discomfort. Again she looked to one side, only to find Jake once more staring at her until he too looked away.

Sally finally stood. "Well, let us go into the dining room. Mother isn't here to greet you all, but Georgiana has cooked a lovely meal. We have Georgiana a few days a week, and she cooks divinely."

Jake waved his hand, gesturing for Olivia to walk before him. He held the chair as she sat down. *A man with manners,* she noted with pleasure. It also signified a man eager to please, which might prove useful to her plans.

As dinner was served, Bodie went into details of the ship's rescue. "So what happened on the boat last night, Jake? What did you see? I never did hear."

Jake cast a glance at Olivia and shook his head. "It's not fitting to go into such details, Bodie. Especially with a situation like this and in the company of one who has already endured so much."

"It's kind of you to think of me, Mr. Harris,"

Olivia said. "But I would very much like to hear what happened. Some say it's better not to remember, but I want to. It's important."

Jake cast her a curious glance but did as she asked. He described the system he used, calling it a breeches buoy. Olivia noticed that he spoke with quiet authority, constantly checking her face to see if his words disturbed her.

"I'm sure Father would have seen such things in use," she commented, buttering a slice of bread.

"Was he in maritime?"

"He was a ship's captain and sailed to many places, mainly in the Caribbean and South America. The crew who sailed with me were all sailors that once worked for him." Her voice drifted away in recollection of the strong, capable men with hearts yearning for adventure. Was Jake that type of man, too? Not that it mattered. The only thing that mattered now was the precious cargo and if he could help save her once again. The small lump that had been in her throat swelled. She quickly grabbed for her glass and sloshed some water onto Jake's lap. "Oh, I'm terribly sorry. How clumsy of me."

"No harm done. We're all familiar with being wet here. I've been in many a storm."

There was a certain strength and matter-of-factness about Jake, like the night of the shipwreck when he held her in the strange apparatus, facing the storm's wrath. Yet he must fear the unknown, and yes, fear he might perish in his manner of work.

"Did you ever consider that you might die while saving those like me?" Olivia suddenly asked.

Both Jake and Bodie put down their forks. A look of panic creased Sally's smooth face, and the ivory color of her skin paled even more.

"No," Jake said. His gaze took on a faraway look for a moment.

"I worry about you all the time, Henry," Sally said to Bodie, poking him in the arm. "I still can't understand why you must go on beach patrol when others can do it."

"He's getting very good at it," Jake added. "A good pair of eyes is needed in this business."

"But Jake has the best eyes," Bodie said. "Either that or he just has a sense about things."

"A sense?" Olivia wondered to Jake. "You mean like a sense of danger?"

Jake shrugged. "I'm not sure what it is. Something comes over me—a feeling that something's wrong. I felt it the night your ship went aground. I like to think that God is telling me when to rescue others."

"He knew you were in trouble, too," Bodie added. "Jake has a sense about a ship in danger."

"Well, I'm grateful for your senses that night. Thank you for risking your lives to save mine." Olivia wiped her lips lightly on her napkin. Yes, this was just the man she needed. One who obviously cared, who had no fear, and who sensed the need of others.

A pie for dessert brought out the best in the men, who both exclaimed their satisfaction over the meal.

Afterward they retired to the sitting room where Jake and Bodie brought out the box they had found. Olivia inhaled a sharp breath when she saw it. Her knees felt weak. With trembling hands she took the box and brought it over to the table. "This is my journal," she said softly. "I kept it inside my personal trunk in the ship's cabin. How did you get it?"

"It washed ashore, didn't it, Bodie?"

The young man nodded. As she slid open the cover to the box, she inquired about any other possessions they had found.

"A few chairs washed up. A small writing table. A sail from the ship. Some boards."

"What do you do with such possessions?"

"Any personal belongings are given to the survivors if they want them," Jake answered. "If not, they are destroyed. Sometimes possessions are kept as evidence if the keeper feels the need."

"The keeper?"

"He is the headmaster or captain of the lifesaving station. He directs the station's activities and the rescues."

Olivia nodded as she drew out the leather journal, none the worse for the storm and seawater thanks to the oilcloth. Her fingers drifted over the leather cover and opened to the page of her last entry before the storm's wrath had claimed their vessel.

I hear O'Malley calling from above deck. He has told me to stay below as the storm has taken a turn for the worse. I know we are not too far distant from Wilmington. If only we can reach a port of safety. But O'Malley says it's impossible. And once more I must pray for this journey, that I will finally see land.

Olivia heaved a sigh and closed her eyes, trying to squelch the rising tears. Instead she concentrated on the matter at hand. "Do you suppose the ship is still afloat?" she wondered aloud.

Jake, who had stood off to one side to allow her time to reflect over the journal she held, now stepped forward. "A section of it is still on the sandbar and..."

Olivia whirled. "Praise be! Please, sir, I ask if you could row me out there to try to retrieve whatever we can. May we leave at first light?"

Jake and Bodie exchanged glances. "Ships in such dire shape as yours are usually left to the will of God. The passengers are normally grateful for their lives. They have little need of cargo."

"I am very thankful for my life. But I will be even more thankful to rescue what we carried in the ship's hold. It's of the utmost importance."

"I—I don't know. I'd have to ask the keeper and..."

"Please secure whatever permissions are necessary, Mr. Harris. I shall be at your station at dawn."

Jake frowned. "I'm unsure if it's safe to return. But if we have permission, Bodie and I will take a surfboat and help. I can ask Grayson, the head surfman, to help as well."

Olivia nodded her head. "I must come, too. Only I know where the cargo is stored. I—I must keep watch over it."

"What's so important about your cargo anyway?" Bodie asked. "What do you carry?"

Olivia glanced at the journal she held. She did not want these men made privy to what she carried in valuable goods and assets. While she wanted to trust them with its contents, the mission to save her brother was too important. If only O'Malley were alive. He would have commanded this retrieval and safeguarded the goods with his life.

"There's no need for us to know personal contents of the cargo, Bodie," Jake hastily intervened. "I will make an attempt to rescue it, Miss Madison, but for certain you will not be allowed to go on this mission."

"I'm not sure why not. It is my vessel after all. But I thank you for your help. It…it means a great deal. More than you know." She managed a smile, realizing she would need to portray a grateful and genteel spirit if she were to rescue what she dearly needed. All she held dear now rested with Jacob Harris.

Jake could not remove the image of flickering blue fire in her eyes or the full red lips that spoke words with equal intensity. Olivia Madison stood straight and commanding before him like the master of her own vessel, despite the dress she wore that outlined her female form. She fought for command of her destiny as well as the fate of her ship. And she was not easily dissuaded, he could tell. Now he must think of a way to convince the keeper to allow him to forgo his duties and see about the woman's cargo, if that were possible.

"I will talk to the keeper," he promised, hoping to see a smile light her lovely face. Instead she turned back to the journal to leaf through more of the entries. He wondered about the journal's contents and what she had witnessed on her long voyage here. He presumed she came from England with her accent, though she never revealed her place of departure. Some hailed from other parts of Europe or from South America. He recalled the ashen look that had come over Olivia's face as she'd silently read her last journal entry, written in fine handwriting. Maybe the words contained fears about the storm. Or the loss of life. He would dearly like to see the entries. But she allowed no one access to the private concerns of her life, made evident by her stubborn interest in locating her precious cargo.

After standing there for a few awkward moments, Jake motioned to Bodie. "I suppose we should be heading back to the station."

"You go on ahead, Jake. I want to say goodbye to Sally."

Jake nodded. He wanted to offer a formal farewell to Olivia Madison, but the words remained stuck in his throat. Instead he glanced around the room for his fisherman's cap tossed in a nearby chair and went to retrieve it.

"I hope you don't think I'm being overly headstrong in wanting to accompany you," Olivia said. "But I have to ensure the cargo is safe."

"No one here is planning to steal your goods, if that is what you fear."

"I fear the ocean will steal them. I want to avoid that at all cost." She stared at him so intently, it appeared as if she had forgotten to blink. Until the long thick lashes did blink, and rather demurely, over a set of sky-blue eyes. He sensed a bond with her somehow. Perhaps it was in the manner of the storm they had endured. Now it looked as if he faced yet another one, with the mysterious cargo in the foundering ship's hold.

"I suppose it makes sense to see your cargo in safe hands," he said. "From the ocean and from others. But I daresay you can trust me, Miss Madison." The words came so swiftly, even he was taken aback by them. Her gaze settled on him, and he saw her nod in agreement.

"I believe I can, sir." Her voice lowered. "By helping me, you are really helping save others. You will prove yourself a true philanthropist. Believe me."

Jake wondered about that comment as he edged his way toward the door. It didn't make sense, but precious little did these days. He took his time retracing the path back to the station. The bright moon shining overhead, coupled with calm winds, provided a good night for ships at sea. He knew in such conditions he would easily be able to see the condition of the woman's vessel beached on the sand bar. Far in the distance he could make out the faint lantern light of a surfman selected for the beach patrol this night. Probably John or Richard were out there and grumbling over the duty that he and Bodie liked so well. He stared for a long time at the ocean but saw just a portion of the vessel, despite the penetrating moonlight. Perhaps the low tide would reveal what was left of the ship and if it was wise to venture out in the surfboat to check for any remaining possessions.

He returned to the station where the men sat around in the common area, sharing stories. The atmosphere was more relaxed without rescues to be made.

"So how was dinner?" Grayson asked.

"Very good. Miss Madison has asked a favor. She wishes to return to her ship tomorrow morning and look for the cargo that was left behind. I suppose from her insistence that the ship carries important merchandise in its hold."

"Did she say what?"

Jake shook his head. "I don't think she trusts us in that respect. But she trusts us enough to go look for it."

Grayson nodded. "I'll help you if the keeper

agrees. And he should. The weather is favorable for a while. We can rest a bit easy."

Jake sighed, knowing that one never truly rests at this job. He would like to, except for the tension rippling across his shoulders and up his neck. Why, he was uncertain. Olivia Madison's insistence in this matter did prove intriguing. Why had she come so far from home, in a boat full of men? And what kind of cargo did she carry?

Chapter 5

Jake had just concluded his devotions and morning prayer in his usual place, on a dune overlooking the ocean, when he heard his name called. He stood, brushing away the sand that collected on his trousers, and closed his Bible. Bodie waved his hand, breathless as he raced up. "Your lady of the sea has arrived, Jake," he announced.

Several had taken to calling Olivia that, as if he and Olivia already shared some special bond. Despite their dinner last evening, she was but a passenger he had delivered from an untimely death. His lady *was* the sea, or so he told himself, and reminded Bodie of that fact.

"Anyway, Miss Madison is back at the station asking for you," Bodie continued. "I guess she wants to go after her cargo."

Jake sighed, wishing she had not come. As it was, he hadn't yet acquired permission of the keeper to take out the surfboat at her request. At least the day at sea proved calm.

Jake followed the anxious Bodie back over the dune and to the station where he saw several figures. He noted one of them appeared slight in frame, wearing a long-sleeve white shirt and trousers. If not for the mane of brown hair wound in a bun behind the nape of the neck, he would have mistaken the figure for any young surfman. Instead Olivia Madison stood outfitted in male attire, determined to be considered one of the crew despite her gender.

"There you are!" Olivia said by way of greeting. "Someone said you were praying. I hope you remembered to pray for success this day."

Jake offered a small smile. He did indeed include Olivia in his prayers, but more importantly, he prayed for God's will in his life.

"She claims she wants to go out after the cargo," Grayson said. "Did you ask permission of the keeper?"

Jake shook his head, which drew a look of consternation from Olivia. "We have no choice," she declared. "I must go before that cargo is lost. There is precious little time."

Just then the keeper himself emerged from the building to inquire of the commotion. When Olivia introduced herself, accompanied by a radiant smile, the man shook her hand politely. "You're looking quite well after all you've been through, Miss Madison."

"Thank you for your help in my rescue. I have a favor to ask. I desperately seek the cargo of my ship before it's washed away."

The keeper shook his head. "I'm sorry, but I'm afraid it's lost."

"Sir, I beg to differ," Jake said, then asked Grayson to lend his spyglass. "If you see, sir, a fair section of ship remains afloat on a sand bar. If we go this morning and the hold is intact, we might be able to retrieve at least part of the cargo."

The keeper surveyed the scene. "And what is so important that I should risk the lives of my men to salvage cargo?"

"This cargo was being brought here to America to save a life," Olivia said. "That's all I can say as the matter is private. But it is no more dangerous than what these men did in risking their lives to save mine the other night. In fact, less so as the seas are calm and the sun is shining."

The keeper frowned. "All right. We have some other rowboats. You can take two with four able-bodied men."

"I can row," Olivia declared.

He shook his head. "I insist you remain here. I cannot risk endangering a passenger on this mission. I will send my men out to recover what they are able to safely. The rest we must leave to the hands of Providence."

Olivia grunted in disappointment. Jake hurried with Bodie to ready a boat. As he worked, he could hear soft breathing close to his ear. The sensation sent goose bumps rising to the surface of his skin. "You must let me come, Jake," a soft voice murmured. He whirled to find Olivia close by, her blue eyes moistened with the makings of an emotional plea.

"I can't. It could mean my job."

"You won't get into trouble." Olivia glanced about and then suddenly darted into the boat, throwing a piece of canvas over her. "I'm a stowaway," her muffled voice came from beneath the canopy. "You don't know I'm on board."

"Jake..." Bodie said in a warning voice. Jake could only shake his head. It made little sense to waste time arguing with the headstrong woman over her devious plans. Instead he and Bodie took up the tow rope and began pulling the boat toward the water's edge, thankful the direction was downhill.

As they tugged on the boat, they found the weight of it sagging in the wet sand. "This isn't gonna work," Bodie whispered fiercely to Jake. "She's going to get us in trouble." He then stared wide-eyed as Grayson ambled over. Jake inhaled a breath, hoping Grayson wouldn't notice the bulky mass under the canvas.

"What, you men get weak all of the sudden?" he joked and helped them maneuver the boat into the water. "I don't recall the boat being this heavy. What's the canvas for?"

"To protect the cargo," Jake said smoothly. "We have no idea what condition it's in."

Grayson nodded and returned to his boat to the sighs of both men, who now took seats and hefted up the oars.

"Thank you," came Olivia's voice. "I owe more than I can pay."

"We'll take whatever you have in that cargo of yours," Bodie joked. The canvas flew aside, revealing Olivia's stern face and eyes that glowered at Bodie.

"I need every stitch of that cargo. And if I've lost any of it, this may be the end."

Jake grunted as he maneuvered the oars. "I don't suppose you could tell us what the cargo is?"

Olivia offered no further explanation to that effect, and Jake let it go, at least for now. Instead he concentrated on maneuvering the boat toward their objective—the damaged schooner barely clinging to the sandbar that had caused the initial wreck. He couldn't help but think of the woman huddled under the canvas. Headstrong and infuriating though she may be, she was also unlike any female he'd ever met. This stretch of sand called Hatteras Island was anything but normal living for a woman. It brought out a ruggedness and independence. But Olivia went far beyond those characteristics, from her forwardness, to her male clothing, to her ability to alter circumstances to her bidding. Every moment brought new revelations about her. Try as he might, he couldn't stop thinking about her.

Once they were safely out in open ocean, Olivia took a seat in the middle of the boat and watched as the shipwrecked vessel came into full view. Jake wondered if memories of the evening's peril filled her mind. As the boats edged closer, Jake could see a good bit of the hull remained intact, though the stern had received significant storm damage. The mainmast had also toppled, not uncommon in violent weather.

"Why, it doesn't look so terrible in the daylight," Olivia observed, the hope clear in her voice. Her eyes glistened with anticipation. "I don't understand how everyone could have died. It doesn't seem possible."

"They may have been tossed overboard," Jake said gently. "In a storm it can easily happen, especially if they were trying to trim the sails. A gust of wind can take hold of the sail and toss the sailor like a rag doll into the sea. I've been in wind like that. There is nothing fiercer than battling wind and wave."

Grayson now drew his boat closer to Jake's and pointed at their third passenger with a scowl. "What in the world is she doing here?" he barked. "Jake, you heard the keeper's orders! She was to remain on shore."

Jake glanced over at Olivia who said nothing. He felt his face heat. "She stowed away under the canvas. She wanted to see what was left of her ship.

By the time she came out of hiding, it was too late to go back."

Grayson frowned, ready to issue a harsh rebuke. He thought on it, shook his head, and set his sights on the matter at hand as they came alongside the damaged vessel. The men anchored the boats so several of them could climb aboard. "This is risky business," Grayson said with a huff as he grabbed hold of a rope and hoisted himself aboard. Olivia maneuvered her way to the edge, ready to climb onto the schooner. "Oh, no, you don't," Grayson charged. "You will stay with the rowboat."

"This is my ship, and I intend to see that my cargo is safely retrieved."

"Then don't ask for another rescue when the ship suddenly gives way and sinks."

Olivia ignored him, climbing aboard with the help of Jake's steady arm and carefully making her way across the slanting deck over protruding boards that had popped from the impact. Jake followed, all the while murmuring a prayer that no calamity would befall them while they were on board.

I am glad to be back on board but sad, too, Olivia thought to herself as she stepped carefully toward the stern of the small vessel that had seen such misfortune. She could still see and hear the effects of the storm: the howling wind, the rain beating down on them, the ship listing in the rough waters. And then she heard the cries for help, the sounds of men shouting as the ship tossed about, the stern commands of O'Malley overshadowed by the fierce grip of the storm. If ever she needed God to give her peace and not abandon her to these memories, now was the time.

"We can't go much farther without risking injury, Miss Madison," Jake warned, his hand gently grabbing hold of her arm to slow her progress. "It appears the ship cracked near the stern when it hit the sand bar."

"We're almost to the hatch. There it is." She pointed to a trap door at mid-deck and, to her dismay, found it secured with a large metal padlock.

"I don't suppose you have a key," Jake said.

Olivia shook her head. "O'Malley had the key for it. I trusted him with everything, and now he is gone." She thought she saw Jake wince and look away. She wondered why but dismissed it. Instead she looked around for some instrument to help break the lock. "If I only had my pistol, I could easily break it open."

"You were armed, too?" Jake said incredulously, scanning her from head to toe as if trying to imagine such a thing.

"Before the storm I was armed, though the men on board never knew it. Of course now the pistol is gone, along with everything else I own. Except for the journal."

"I've never known a woman to carry a gun."

"Don't you think a woman should be able to protect herself from rogues and scoundrels? Though I can hardly say I was in any danger with the fine sailors who gave their lives to see me safely here to America. But I do wonder about your homeland here, sir, and if a woman should be armed for protection. I daresay few women grace this coast in America."

"There are not many," he admitted, finding a thick chain and beginning to beat at the lock with a grunt. "I'm not sure this will do." Grayson came over to add another large iron pick and together he and Jake managed to crack the padlock. When they did, the ship lurched. Olivia would have lost her footing if not for Jake, who grabbed her arm to steady her. The swift touch brought back memories of that night during the rescue, when his strong arms bore her up inside the strange contraption that dragged her to safety. She tried not to react to his touch but couldn't help feeling a sudden warmth.

"We don't have much time," Grayson said. "I think this is a dangerous scheme, miss. You'll end up in the water before you set eyes on your precious cargo, if the cargo hold hasn't already flooded. This is not worth our lives."

"Then by all means save your life, sir, if it is that valuable to you. I intend to see what remains." She knew her comment would draw a look of consternation, but she was willing to endure it all to see the cargo safely to shore. Olivia peered into the dark, dismal hold that reeked of rotting fish. Several rats scurried out, relieved to be set free. She could see the sunlight reflecting on water as black as night and several large crates still housed within. "It's here!" she exclaimed, unable to contain her joy. "Blessed be! I knew it would be all right. At least a good deal of cargo appears intact from what I can tell. There's some water in the hold but not much."

Grayson was already outfitting a pulley and heavy rope he found to help hoist the crates out of the hold. Jake carefully entered the hold and secured the roping. When it was ready, they obliged Richard and Bodie to leave their boats and come help. Olivia stood by in expectation, her heart pounding in her chest, as the men worked together to hoist the wooden crates, one at a time, to the deck. There had been six in all when they boarded the ship at Portsmouth. When the first crate came up under the sweat dripping from the men's brows and staining their shirts, she clapped her hands. "Wonderful!"

"These are heavy and cumbersome," Grayson noted gruffly. "It's going to take more than mere rowboats to see them to shore. And I don't know how much longer this ship will stay afloat, either. We've been lucky so far."

"Mr. Wilson owns a fishing vessel," Jake suggested. "We can ask to borrow his boat to transport them."

The next two crates were small enough that Grayson decided they could be rowed safely to shore. Olivia patted each one as if she had found long-lost family members. In a way she had. If the water had not damaged the contents, they would be used by her uncle to help Nathan. How she wanted to check on the condition of the items by opening the crates, but she refrained for now. There would be plenty of time once safely back on shore and reunited with her uncle before inspecting the items. She didn't want others knowing what they contained. She refused to trust anyone. Trust these days was hard to find, though she had to muster a bit of trust in these men who came to help her. Especially in the one in which she had first trusted her life.

She ran her hand across the rough wood of the crates, thinking of Jake's willingness to help, even allowing her to venture to the ship against the orders of his superior. Maybe she could trust Jake with the contents. Maybe his trust was what she dearly needed to see this safely delivered to Uncle Dwight in Raleigh.

Jake held out his hand to assist her off the vessel. "We need to see about securing another boat."

Olivia shook her head, though she clearly heard his request. She felt his steady gaze from a set of dark brown eyes. "I don't want to leave the rest of the crates behind."

"Well, you can't stay here alone," Grayson snapped. "This ship is highly unstable and could sink at any moment."

"Then if I go down with the ship, it's my own foolhardiness. But I will not leave my cargo."

Grayson muttered something to the effect of her

obstinacy equaling that of an ox before directing Richard and Bodie to take one of the boats and find out if the Wilson fishing vessel was available. "The two of you can take the other rowboat and its contents to shore, and I will remain with the cargo."

Olivia pondered this, wondering if she should accept the suggestion even as Grayson frowned in disdain. "You can't guard your cargo in two places, miss," he added with a raw chortle.

"I trust Jake with the rowboat, but I will remain here until all the pieces are safely aboard the other vessel."

"No, you won't," Grayson said with a growl.

"Yes, I will!" Her hands flew to her hips, and her foot stomped on the deck to emphasize the point.

"I suppose it takes a strong will to have made it this far, Miss Madison," Grayson grunted. "But this goes beyond me, and I am a God-fearing man that usually understands things. You, woman, I do not understand. Your obstinacy vastly outweighs my patience."

Olivia whirled and stared out to sea, not wishing to debate the matter further.

"Grayson, you go ahead and row the smaller crates back to shore," Jake suggested. "If Miss Madison insists on staying, I don't want to leave her alone out here. And the keeper may need you for some other business. You are surfman number one."

"I suppose it's better you were the one to volunteer," he said grimly, taking hold of the rope to ease himself back down to the rowboat. "If it were me with her, one of us would have ended up in the hold where the cargo once was." With a grunt he took up the oars and began rowing back toward the mainland.

Olivia and Jake remained on the ship that continued to list precariously. Jake looked about, sizing up the situation with a practiced eye, as if he had seen many vessels in such a condition. "I'm amazed this boat hasn't sunk," he said. "God must have wanted to see your cargo safely delivered."

"At least this is one prayer the Almighty has answered. I've not had many requests reach heaven these days."

"All our prayers reach God's ears. Sometimes His answer is different than ours. Sometimes it's no."

"No, is it? No to sparing lives? No to calming a terrible storm? Didn't even the Savior Christ command the winds and sea obey Him and be made calm? Didn't His disciples cry out for help, and He heard them?"

"He told them to have faith. You need faith too, Miss Madison. Faith in God's sovereignty despite what you see or understand."

Olivia had no words to counter Jake's matter-of-factness or the confidence with which he spoke. This resolute surfman was more than he seemed at first glance, giving fire to pious words that could not be quenched by any human reply. She now waited along with Jake, praying that the boats would soon return before the schooner breathed its last.

Chapter 6

Olivia waited as patiently as she could muster for the boats to come take her and the cargo to safety but Jake's words had rattled her. She often thought herself a respectable lady and a believer of Scripture but all that had been put into question since her arrival here.

Father had always admonished her not to judge who she was—that God had made her unique and with special talents. She now had to wonder at those words, looking at the tattered pants with rips at the knee, and the soiled shirt far too big for her slight frame. It all looked so unbecoming to a woman, she knew, along with her staunch ways that irritated Grayson.

At least she found a bit of a confidant in Jake, who

did not appear to criticize her. From the moment he rescued her, she felt he understood her far better than any other man here. Maybe it was his strong Christian character that drove his actions. He respected her for who she was. He acknowledged her concerns. He had arranged for the rescue of the cargo and allowed her to be a part of the mission over Grayson's objections. She believed she could trust him more and more with each passing hour.

But now the man paced back and forth, growing nervous the longer they remained on the ill-fated ship. Occasionally he studied the sky and the cloud patterns, testing the wind as well before resuming his anxious pacing.

"I hope they return soon," Jake finally said. "I don't like the look of the clouds. I've seen such patterns before, and they usually signal a change in the weather and a shift in the wind's direction."

Olivia could not help a sudden chill from overcoming her, making her teeth rattle. "I—I hope you're mistaken," she managed to blurt out through trembling lips.

"I'm sorry, I didn't mean to frighten you. I've seen this before. And ships that are ripped apart on the shoals such as yours are easily swept away if the wind picks up."

Olivia shuddered at the vision of the ship losing its precarious grip on the sandbar before foundering and sinking. She vividly recalled the frigid water. During the rescue her feet and legs had turned to useless stumps of flesh by the time Jake had brought her safely to shore. It did not spur confidence for survival if they suddenly found themselves in the steely, gray-blue ocean.

"It will be all right," he assured her. "Trust in the Almighty."

"You say that, but who is to know when the Almighty might decide you are better off as food for the fish?"

Jake looked once more to the sky. "I don't pretend to understand everything He decides to do. Nor do I understand why He took my brother."

Olivia unfolded her arms and stared at him. "You lost your brother?"

He flinched and didn't answer, pretending instead to look around the ship for something as yet unseen.

He should understand my predicament in needing to save Nathan! "This is why I risk everything for the voyage." She pointed to the cargo. "In these crates are items that can be sold to help free my brother."

"What did he do?"

"He committed no crime. A scoundrel of a business partner stole the company money. Nathan could not pay the debt. He was cast into debtor's prison until he could pay back what he owed."

"And you plan to pay the debt with the cargo you carry?"

"Yes. Nathan is not only my brother but my last living family member other than my uncle. I will do whatever it takes to see him set free."

"I'm not certain what God would think of such a desperate act. He asks you have faith in Him rather than in your own devices."

Olivia shook her head. "I'm not sure that God is listening to me anyway. Otherwise, why would He let such terrible events happen?"

"God is a Comforter, a Guide, and a Strength. And a Friend, too. Jesus called His disciples friends. He even went on to say that those who listened to His words were his mother and brothers. It's right to call the Almighty a tried-and-true Friend in times of need."

Olivia found herself speechless. She'd never heard anyone speak as Jake did, though the reverend in her congregation in England often spoke of God in matters of life. She wished then she had not ignored the sermons he gave when she was younger. "I have a difficult time believing He is a Friend. Maybe one day I can believe like you do."

"So, you are not a Christian?"

His words came like a direct blow to her spirit. "Yes I am. I have attended church. I speak about God. I have been baptized and bear a Christian name, though I use my given name. I pray, though He doesn't seem to hear."

"Is God also a part of your every being? Everything you are and everything you hope to be? Is He Lord of all through Christ His Son?"

Olivia opened her mouth, ready to agree, before clamping it shut. And just as swiftly the boat lurched under a sudden burst of wind. She grabbed hold of the railing as did Jake. The boat groaned as if in pain, along with the distant sound of splintering wood. "Oh, no! Are we tearing apart, Jake?" Her voice quaked.

"I don't know." He managed to make his way toward the aft of the vessel where part of the deck had broken away. "We are still on the sandbar, but if the water increases below deck, we will either be set adrift or sink."

The vessel shuddered once more. Suddenly Jake was hurled overboard. Her arms flailed and a shout of surprise burst from his lips as he plunged into the foaming water below. Olivia screamed and hurried to the railing. All she could see was frothing ocean waves. Panic assailed her. "Jake! Jake! Oh, no! Dear God, no. Jake, can you hear me?" After a frantic moment, she saw him emerge from the depths, bobbing in the water.

"Th-throw me some r-rope!" he sputtered, furiously treading salt water to stay afloat. Olivia searched the deck and, finding a coil of rope, tossed the end out to him with all her might. "Oh, God, if ever I needed strength for a task, please grant me strength with this." With a shout she grabbed hold of the rope and began to heave, fighting against the massive strength of the current that held Jake in a watery grip. The damp rope began slipping through her hands. "Jake, I'm losing you!" she cried, sensing her helplessness.

He swam bravely against the current and then found some broken boards jutting from the ship's gunwale. Slowly he dragged himself up, water streaming off his saturated clothing and hair. He flung himself up and over to the deck where he collapsed in exhaustion, his breathing labored.

"Jake, are you all right?" Olivia knelt beside him. She heard his still-rapid breathing while she pushed back wet hair and wiped water droplets from his face with the tattered edge of her shirt. Thankfulness filled her, as did relief mixed with admiration. "You're such a strong swimmer," she marveled. "Praise be."

"A good thing I am." He caught his breath and slowly sat up. "But we haven't much time before this ship is lost. W-we should have never stayed behind."

"It will be all right."

He slowly climbed to his feet, the exhaustion evident as he staggered along the deck. "The cargo is lost, Olivia. You will need to make other arrangements to help gain your brother's freedom. When those boats return, we are abandoning the vessel. Our lives are more important than possessions."

Seeing him affected by the ravages of the sea that nearly claimed his life, she struggled to find her determination. "I know it seems hopeless. But I could not have come this far to abandon what I worked so hard to achieve. Others gave their lives to see the cargo to its final destination. You are also a man of faith, Mr. Harris. Where is your faith now?"

He pushed back locks of wet hair from his face. "My faith also means trusting in sound decisions with the mind the Almighty gave me. Trying to rescue your cargo has put lives at risk."

"Tell me this then. If you were able to rescue your brother with the cargo you carried, would you do everything in your strength to save it?" She watched a ripple of pain cross his features. She didn't know the true circumstances surrounding the brother he had lost, but she prayed that somehow his heart would realize the importance of this mission, even unto death.

"How can you ask me that?" he lashed out. "It makes no difference now."

"You told me you had lost a brother, and so I thought you might sympathize with..."

"You don't know my situation. I did all I could the day of his death. And right now I've had my fill of rescuing petty possessions and arguing with a foolish woman." He wiped his face with his soggy shirtsleeve and walked away.

"You'll save lives in your breeches buoy, but you won't save the cargo that can set an innocent man free. Maybe your rescuing is more for personal glory than true assistance in times of need." Once Olivia said it, she instantly regretted it. But she had little choice. Jake had been her rescuer at sea and with the cargo. She needed his help. She only prayed she had not pushed him away. If she had, she may well have dealt a death blow to the only hope left to securing her brother's freedom. "I'm sorry I spoke so harshly," she said quickly. "Forgive me."

Jake said nothing but continued walking to the other side of the deck. Now Olivia could only watch and wait as clouds massed on the distant horizon. She prayed the storm would stay away and not hamper the men returning for them. They would not be abandoned, though she did wonder what was taking the men so long.

Another jolt nearly sent Olivia sprawling to the deck below. Fear clawed at her. Maybe Jake was right. Maybe she had been foolish to place all her hopes in mere cargo and not in God's provision. To her, the cargo was God's answer—a heavenly gift from those who gave their wealth to help Nathan. Maybe she needed to look to other avenues short of selling herself as some indentured servant to pay off old debts.

At last she caught sight of two boats, one large and one small, making their way toward their ailing ship. Jake saw it too and came portside to await their arrival. He said nothing to her but only stood fast, ready to receive the lines to secure the crafts as best he could alongside the vessel. Grayson and Bodie had returned along with Richard. To Olivia's dismay, the head surfman, Grayson, still possessed the same frown on his face he wore when he left. The look must bolster Jake's opinion, that this was mere folly. But she pushed it aside to concentrate on the cargo.

"What happened to you, Jake?" Bodie wondered

aloud when he saw Jake standing there in dripping clothes with a puddle of water forming at his feet.

"I took a swim."

The men looked at each other until he explained how the wind jostled the ship and sent him overboard.

"Don't you know how to keep to your feet, man?" Richard said in jest.

"I nearly didn't have time to come back," Grayson added, his face grim. "We've got an important visitor coming soon, and the keeper is not happy that we are out rescuing this cargo."

"Who?" Jake wondered.

"Someone from the staff of Superintendent Kimball of the lifesaving service is set to arrive and inspect the station. You remember the fellow from last year's visit, Jake?"

"I remember." He cast a glance at Olivia.

"We need to get back as soon as possible. The keeper wants to run a beach apparatus drill, and the station has to be cleaned from top to bottom. There's too much at stake not to be fully ready."

Jake cast another irritated glance at Olivia as if she were a disruption to their plans and their station. She ignored it and watched the last of the cargo being loaded safely onto the main boat. Jake offered her a hand down into a boat but she ignored it and carefully used the rope to ease herself into the fishing vessel that carried the cargo. Now all she needed to do was contact her uncle in Raleigh and have him come for her. She would heartedly give these men her thanks and persuade Uncle to give them some money. But once she left, she planned never to lay eyes on this place again. Nor would she give further consideration to her rescuer.

What more could happen? Jake thought with a silent groan as he fought against the current seeking to take them off course rather than toward the station. Not only did he have to contend with this situation of Olivia Madison, but now the lifesaving board was planning another impromptu visit to the humble station. Everyone would be frantic. Superintendent Kimball was a hard man who wanted the best, most proficiently run lifesaving service along the Atlantic seaboard. Jake recalled the surprise visit last season. When the board member noted equipment in ill condition and laggardness among the surfmen, the keeper did whatever was required to rid the station of its ills. Several surfmen lost their jobs. The board member even threatened to close the station if things did not improve. Jake only prayed that Olivia Madison's foolhardy errand did not now jeopardize their station's livelihood.

Olivia. She had already tested him well beyond his Christian forbearance. Though he had to admit, with the wind tugging her hair out of its chignon and sending it in a flurry the color of brown sugar about her shoulders, she did appear attractive sitting in the boat. But just as quickly, her hands grabbed hold of the offending mane, twisting it into a knot and tucking it back in its rightful place, as if the outward sign of womanhood was not welcome. Jake frowned. Olivia gave the semblance of one who fought against the societal norms of a lady—wearing men's clothing, joining the dangerous mission to save the cargo from a sinking ship, carrying a pistol, journeying thousands of miles from her native land. But really, she had left it all for her own lifesaving cause. He couldn't blame her for her insistence on helping save her brother. Jake could not help his own brother, Thomas, when he'd needed Jake the most. The painful memories had been shut up in his heart until Olivia came and broke open the lock.

Soon they approached the beach, where they all jumped into the cold ocean water and used the tow ropes to drag the boats to shore. Olivia inquired about a wagon and horses to help transport the cargo back to the home where she was staying. Jake sighed and glanced at Grayson, who gave a harsh look as if he'd rather not be involved any longer in this mission.

The surfman John arrived from the station. "The keeper needs you all for the drill," John announced breathlessly, stopping short when he saw Olivia and the stack of crates. "What do you have in there anyway?"

"My trousseau of course," she announced. "The best England has to offer. Surely frocks of a sort would not interest a robust man like you."

John frowned in disgust and strode off. Jake

couldn't help but smile and suddenly saw Olivia smiling in return. This was a part of her he'd seen only in glimmers. She had only ever been obstinate in this venture. Hard. Cold and calculating. Using men, including him, to do her bidding. He then recalled the time on the ship when he fell overboard. She could also be caring. Dutiful. Determined. Maybe even compassionate. Now she sauntered toward him, pushing back a portion of her brown mane that had again fallen out of its chignon.

"I hope you will forgive the words I said on board the ship," she said, her voice like a gentle breeze instead of a wind-driven tempest. "I only wanted to get the cargo to shelter in case that storm did blow up. I'm not one to easily give up. Thank you for your help. Now if there is some way to get it to town…"

Jake had been nervously eyeing the station and the men who even now were readying the equipment for a practice drill. Grayson looked his way and waved his hand for him to come. "Miss Madison, I can't help any more with this endeavor. I am needed at the station. Perhaps you could hire a horse, wagon and men in town to bring up the cargo." He left her but sensed her piercing gaze following him. As he told himself once before, lifesaving must come first. Until Olivia's words on board the ship echoed in his thoughts. *Maybe your rescuing is more for personal glory than true assistance in times of need.*

Jake arrived just as the men were readying the lines for the drill. The keeper gave him a frosty look but ordered Jake to man the Lyle gun, to his surprise. Normally the keeper did it himself, but it wasn't uncommon in a drill that he assigned the task to other surfmen in case one or more of them became incapacitated. All must know the various functions of the rescue operations, and today the Lyle gun fell to Jake. Jake hated operating it as he had little practice firing any weapon, let alone a miniature cannon. He'd rather do the duty he believed he did best—rescuing passengers via the breeches buoy. But he stood ready with John on the other side of the tiny gun, awaiting the commands.

"Looks like you and your lady of the sea are getting along well," John murmured. "I heard Grayson say you and her were on the ship for a while. A good long while in fact. Alone." He emphasized the point.

"And what does that matter…?" Jake began.

"It matters a lot when one…"

"Ready!" the call came.

Jake ignored John and positioned the gun to hit the target presented in the water. But then something jostled the gun's placement just as the order came to fire. The projectile sailed left and well past the target, to the jeers of the other surfmen.

"Surfman number three, what are you doing?" the keeper shouted.

"Sir, his mind is still out there on the ship with his lady of the sea," John remarked with a chuckle.

Jake whirled and before he realized what he was doing, struck John in his laughing face with a balled fist. The man sprawled into the sand. The other surfmen stared in horror, first at the pair and then at the keeper, whose face turned cherry red. The keeper hurried over. "Surfman number three, you are hereby dismissed from the drill. Report to my office later."

Jake grabbed for his cap that had flown off and strode away, but not before glancing at Olivia, who had witnessed the whole thing. Though his anger burned hot, he saw something on her face he thought he would never see.

Compassion.

Chapter 7

The rest of the day saw the other surfmen hard at work, practicing the beach apparatus drill over and over to the satisfaction of the keeper, who manned the Lyle gun. Jake kept to himself inside the station while the men remained outside with the tasks at hand. He flexed his swollen hand, wondering what on earth had possessed him to do such a thing as strike a fellow surfman. He knew quite well the verses in Scripture having to do with self-control. Yet he felt on edge. The ribbing by John had set him off like a match to a firecracker. Now he worried the ensuing explosion might have cost him his job.

When the men filed back inside, exclaiming over the activities of the day, Jake tried to disappear into a back corner until he heard Grayson call his name.

At first Jake wasn't certain he wanted to answer but finally ventured out to meet whatever fate awaited him.

"The keeper wants to see you."

Jake nodded and strode purposefully out of the room. He stopped short when he felt a hand on his arm. He turned to face Grayson. "Jake, I'm not going to tell you that John probably had that coming to him," he said in a low voice. "I mean, you know it in your heart. Things have been tense around here, and now with a committee person arriving in a matter of days, everyone is very nervous. Don't push yourself to the brink over any of this, and least of all over John. I'd hate to lose you. You're a good worker, and lives depend on your skill."

"I wonder if that is true anymore," he muttered. "It's making me think more and more that none of this is worth it. Losing my fiancée, seeing people turn against me, including the keeper, facing John and his schemes…"

"Of course lives are worth it, and you know it. For sure that young lady we helped wouldn't be alive today if you hadn't gone out to get her. And just to let you know, I already told the keeper that John had intentionally disrupted the Lyle gun so it missed its mark. He isn't going to brand you or anything. Just don't say or do anything you'll regret."

"Thanks, Grayson." He walked out of the room, past the curious faces of the men who gathered in the living quarters. John mumbled something under his breath while Richard and Bodie just stared. Jake ignored it all and went straight for the keeper's study. Inside the room the man, normally busy at his desk, now paced the floor. When Jake entered, the keeper sighed and pointed to a chair.

"You won't believe how much trouble we'll be in if this situation is not cleared up, Mr. Harris."

"Sir?"

"This trouble between you and surfman number four. I spoke with Grayson, and he told me the man maliciously moved the gun during the drill. Why are you two having difficulties? We're about to be inspected by a member of the bureau any day, and now you decide to pick a quarrel. That can't happen, not on my watch or anyone's."

"I'm very sorry, sir, but he had it coming to him. I couldn't take it."

"Even if he did, do you realize that such action wounds our ranks? We're supposed to work together, not tear each other apart. Only as a team can we save lives. I hope you will do whatever it takes to mend this breach, young man. And above all, practice self-control." He paused. "I've heard rumors, you know. What happened up at Pea Island and how the board dismissed the entire station crew for disorderly conduct. The superintendent insists that these stations are run properly. We could all be out of a job if he finds otherwise." The keeper paused. "There's even been talk they might close this station once the new station is operational near the Hatteras lighthouse.

They talked about it at a meeting of the head keepers. If we don't do our jobs, we won't be here much longer."

"But we just opened this station a few years ago! We are doing our jobs and with great skill. They need this station on this part of the coast. It's the closest to the Diamond Shoals. We have a young lady who's alive today because of the efforts of this station. Every surfman performed his duty that night."

"It may not be enough."

Jake paused until a thought occurred to him. "Having an eyewitness account would put to rest any misgivings the superintendent or anyone else might have. If you want, sir, I can ask Miss Madison if she would give testimony of our professionalism the night of the rescue."

The keeper thought on it before nodding. "That's an interesting idea. We've never had an actual passenger give a firsthand account to the board. That might prove helpful if it can be arranged."

Jake breathed easier at the thought he may have provided the keeper a way to promote the station and also soothe the tension surrounding his altercation with John. When he left the room, confidence swelled within him, even as his fellow surfmen gazed at him in curiosity.

"So what happened?" Richard asked, pouring coffee from a pot on the stove. "Have you been dismissed? If so, we'll all move up in rank, I gather."

"No, I'm still here." He gave a sideways glance at

John. "And we're going to show that man from the bureau what excellent service we provide here at the station. If we don't, we'll lose our jobs for sure."

At this the men stopped what they were doing and set their sights on him. Jake sat down in a chair, not even concerned for the look of anger on John's face or the welt still visible on the man's cheekbone from the harsh encounter on the beach.

"What are you saying?" asked Richard.

"I heard it directly from the keeper. If we don't pass inspection, they could dismiss us all and even close down the station."

"They can't do that!" Bodie exclaimed. "Why, the station's only been going a few years."

"They can do whatever they want. Look at what happened at Pea Island. The whole crew was ordered to leave. So we have to work together. And that means..." Jake drew in a sharp breath. "I'm sorry for hitting you, John. Can we shake hands and forget this happened? We need to work together and not be at odds." He held out his hand.

The man stared. "I'm not sorry. You think you're one of the best surfmen here, even if you're only one rank higher than me. You shouldn't be. The next time we send out the breeches assembly, I'll be the one commanding it, not you." He strode off, even as the surfmen shook their heads in dismay.

"It's okay, Jake," Bodie said. "We're all in this together, and we know it."

Jake found comfort in the words of his young

friend but at the same time felt a certain disquiet when it came to the unpredictable surfman number four, John Hastings. Again he couldn't dwell on it. He had important matters to tend to, chief of which was coming to friendly terms with the obstinate Olivia Madison. He promised the keeper he'd have her testimony for the bureau. Now he must coax her back to an amiable side, which he hoped would be easy to do. After all Jake believed she cared. She was beholden to them. Not only had she been rescued, but her cargo, too. And he'd caught a glimpse of sympathy on her fine features after the incident with John during the drill. He hoped she remained sympathetic and would agree to offer good words to the board member on behalf of their activities. Little did Olivia Madison know, but the future of the station might well rest in her hands.

Olivia sat at the writing desk inside the small room Sally and her mother had provided her. Earlier that day she had helped with some menial tasks as well as chatting with them about life in England. Sally appeared intrigued by Olivia's descriptions of her family—Father's duties at sea, Mother, who weaved beautiful artistry into fine tapestries and was even asked to help decorate the palace in London, and then Nathan's false imprisonment that spurred this journey to America. Sally was particularly intrigued by the descriptions of the journey here out in the open sea for nearly a month.

"I don't know how you did it," she remarked, her hazel eyes large with wonder. "I could never see myself alone on a ship with rough sailors. It's so unseemly. Not to mention sailing across a dangerous ocean."

"I did have my maid with me," Olivia said in defense. The mention of the sweet blond-haired Alicia sparked a dewy-eyed remembrance of yet another life lost. Looking down at the paper where she was constructing a letter to her uncle, she thought of composing some message to Alicia's parents in England, telling them of the tragedy. And she needed to let the families of the sailors know of their fate as well. But she didn't know how she could relay such messages of grief and feared her tears would stain the papers.

Olivia sighed. She would save those sad tasks for another time and continue the important communication to her uncle. After writing the final sentence, she sat back to read it.

Dearest Uncle,
I write this to announce my arrival to America and North Carolina, but under the saddest of situations. The ship I was on encountered a terrifying storm and all were lost. But through the courageous efforts of a lifesaving crew here at a station on this place called Hatteras Island, I was rescued and so too was the cargo.

I beseech you, dear Uncle, to come quickly so I might deliver the goods to you and hasten

Nathan's release from the prison. I am staying at the home of a Mrs. Dorothea Hamilton of Hatteras Village and her daughter, Sally.

I am your obedient servant and grateful niece,

Olivia Grace Madison of Wiltshire

Olivia signed her name with a flourish and folded it. She hoped within a few weeks Uncle Dwight would arrive, and she would be finished with this sad part of her life. What once began as a noble venture with kindhearted, eager souls had turned into a never-ending nightmare. Peace seemed so far away, it may as well have been a distant star in the night sky. She longed for the comfort of family, even if it was with a distant uncle.

Olivia decided then that an evening walk tonight among the stars might be nice, once she finished this communication. She would enjoy the ocean breezes and try to conjure up hope for peace and safety here in a strange land, at least temporarily. It would take time and money, along with favorable weather, to return to England, bearing the money Nathan needed. She would see to his freedom. Then there were further decisions to be made. Where to live. What to do.

She glanced down at her ill-fitting attire and the sleeves that even now interfered at times with her writing. After losing her trunk in the shipwreck, Olivia longed for a decent dress and other personal possessions. Maybe Uncle would fetch fair prices on the goods and there would be money to spare for a gown and hat.

Olivia pushed aside the letter and drew forward the leather journal. How thankful she was to have this important piece of the journey. God had seen it safely sent via the waters to be picked up by Sally's beau. In it were a great many secrets. Hopes. Dreams. And yes, fears.

Now she opened it to write yet another entry. The last one described the events of securing the cargo, from hiding in the boat to the time on board the ship with Jake, to the delivery of the cargo that still remained in the storehouse at the lifesaving station. She prayed it was safe from harm. She thought of bringing it back here for safekeeping but realized quickly there was no room. Storage in town would cost money which she didn't have. Reluctantly she left it at the station for the time being, assured by the man named Grayson that they could keep it for a brief time while she awaited her uncle's arrival.

"Olivia!"

Olivia heard her name and promptly stood to her feet. "Yes?"

Sally appeared, her face all smiles. "You have a caller. He's waiting in the sitting room."

Who in the world could be calling on her? Her heart began to flutter. Perhaps by some miracle Uncle Dwight had received news of her arrival. Maybe the station had wired him of her whereabouts. Though when she considered it, she'd shared no information about her uncle to the crew. Then again, her memory proved faulty these days.

Olivia hastened from the room and down the hallway, stopping short before the sitting room to see Jake standing there, thumbing through the Hamilton family Bible that rested on a table. She observed him silently. How different he appeared compared to when they last saw each other on board the ill-fated schooner. He had been fairly drenched from his abrupt encounter with ocean. She had been dressed in trousers, her hair a tangled mess, but her spirit fierce and determined. Memories of the quarrel they'd had on board rose up. Then the incident on the shore when Jake struck a fellow surfman, revealing a different side of his nature she never would have believed. She stepped back. He was not always a genteel soul. In fact, their changes in demeanor proved strikingly similar.

He turned, and their gazes met. "Miss Madison," he said, swiping off his fisherman's cap and bowing swiftly.

"Mr. Harris. To what do I owe this visit?" She swept into the room and to a chair where she found a seat.

"I wanted to see how you fared. And to ask a small favor."

Olivia raised her eyebrow in interest. What could he possibly want with her? She had enough troubles of her own. "I'm doing quite well, all things considered. Your Mr. Grayson found a temporary place to store my cargo in one of the station's sheds. I do hope it's well."

"I don't know, but I can find out."

"I hope so. It means the world to me, as you well know." She paused. "What is it you want?"

Jake inhaled a deep breath. He stood in silence as if trying to muster the words to speak then went and sat down. "I don't know if you've heard, but we have a very important member from the lifesaving board coming to inspect the station soon. The keeper wants the station in tip-top shape. A favorable review will keep the station and its activities intact. This is really a matter of life or death."

"I did hear something about it when your friends returned to help us move the cargo. What do you mean by a matter of life or death?"

Jake began twisting the cap in his hands. "Let's just say this board member holds the key to this station's survival. He will report back to the superintendent with his opinion on whether our efforts are worthy enough to keep the station open. Rumor has it he may shut down the station if we do not meet with his expectations."

"I'm sorry to hear that. I'm not certain what I can do to help."

Jake straightened in his chair. "You can do a great deal for us, Miss Madison. If you would agree to serve as a witness of our operations when the board member arrives and tell him what happened the night of the rescue. I asked the keeper, and he thought it was an excellent suggestion."

"I don't remember much of that night, in all honesty. I don't know how I can help. I'm sorry."

He twisted his mouth in dismay. "What about the cargo?"

"Unfortunately, the entire time I was out there retrieving the cargo, I felt as if I were waging a war with you men just to take back what was rightfully mine. I asked for help and received hardship instead."

Jake stood to his feet. "You do remember we nearly lost our lives trying to save your cargo. In fact, I nearly drowned." He turned away. "I apologize. I was hoping for help, but I can see I was in error."

"Mr. Harris, I'm grateful for your help. If you wish me to say that to your visitor, I will. But anything else would not be truthful. As a pious man, I'm sure you would agree that a lie is not worth gambling with the station's reputation."

Jake flinched and suddenly, to her surprise, he sat back down. "I don't want you to say anything but the truth. I only want to go on serving this station and saving lives like your own. I don't want them to take that away from us. People will die because of it. I hope you can understand that."

His mellow voice was like balm dripping over her. She saw before her one who desperately loved what he did. One who wanted to help others above all else. And one who felt himself sinking, as she once felt on that ill-fated ship. "Of course I will do whatever I can," she said softly. "I owe you everything."

His gaze met hers and the frown lines were quickly replaced with the quivering lines of a smile. "Thank you, Olivia."

A tremor raced through her at the sound of her name uttered from his lips. "I wrote to my uncle, telling him what happened. I'm hoping he will come soon."

"I hope so, too. It's been a long journey. You need a place of security and peace."

Her heart warmed at his words. "That's exactly what I was thinking. How much I need peace. I—I haven't felt it in so long, I can barely remember."

"Jesus said He would give us peace. Not as the world gives, but as He gives. I know I need that peace in my life. Not…" He hesitated, his face coloring. "Not like the brawl you witnessed on the beach the other day. I need to be one able to control his actions and trust God for his life."

Olivia found herself strangely endeared to his words and possibly even to the man himself. They both looked at each other until Jake unraveled his cap and placed it on his head. Olivia giggled when she saw the misshapen form of the hat now perched on his head. "Look what you did to your hat, Jake!" she said with a laugh, gesturing him to the mirror.

He chuckled. "It will flatten out in no time."

"When will you need me to bear witness to your official?"

"When he arrives, which should be soon. Thank you again for offering to share a testimony."

Olivia nodded and watched him exit. When he did, Sally appeared from the opposite room. "I thought he would stay to tea."

"You know the surfmen. They are always on duty."

Sally nodded. "Always. And they love it so."

Olivia could plainly see that during the conversation with Jake. The love for his job went beyond comprehension, despite the danger. It left her curious and intrigued and took her admiration to new heights. It must be a similar courage which grips men in the fervor of battle, unafraid for their lives, doing what must be done to secure victory, even if it meant death. Jake had met the battle of the ocean face-to-face, determined to secure victory despite the long odds. He had been there for her when she needed him most. He deserved all the help she could give and more when these superiors came on their inspection. Dare she try to consider opening her heart to him as well?

Chapter 8

Olivia appeared for breakfast the next day to find Sally humming a song, dressed in a frilled apron while putting out freshly baked blueberry muffins. Sunday was Georgiana's day off.

Mrs. Hamilton was there too, having returned last night after spending several days visiting her sister. She bubbled over with news, exclaiming about the people busy with their affairs, the health of the relatives and how immaculate the house appeared. When she saw Olivia, she smiled while slowly pinning her hair into a fashionable bun and inquired how she was. "Sorry I had to leave so soon after you were brought in. But I knew Sally would take care of you."

"I'm doing very well, thank you," she said. "I am posting a letter to my uncle tomorrow in the hopes he will come fetch me as soon as possible. I don't wish to be a burden."

"Stay as long as you like. From what Sally has told me, you've been a great help here. And she enjoys the company. As you can imagine, there aren't many young ladies her age in Hatteras Village. But plenty of rough men. At least I do rather like that young man she talks to. Henry is his name. He has a respectable profession working at the lifesaving station."

Olivia thought back to the harsh exchange she'd witnessed between Jake and the other surfman on the beach. It wasn't all respectable but in fact could be quite rough, more so than she might have imagined. Her father would never have accepted such behavior among his crew. At least it was gratifying to know that Jake was sorry for what had happened. She owed a debt of gratitude to them for her safety and the safety of the cargo. She only prayed that when the time came for the inspection of the station by the lifesaving board, it would go well for them and her testimony would help secure their standing.

Olivia took a place at the breakfast table, joined by Mrs. Hamilton, who wore a fashionable gown as if ready for an evening affair. "I trust you are coming to church services with us today?" she wondered.

The invitation took Olivia by surprise. "Church services?"

"Of course. Today is Sunday. Surely you are a Christian?"

"Oh, I went to church, yes, but not in many weeks,

what with the ocean voyage." Olivia felt warm when the older woman fixed her gaze on her.

"Surely there was a chaplain on board."

"Not on our tiny vessel." She faltered when the woman's gaze hardened into a look of disdain. "I recall reading the Bible. Our first mate, O'Malley, sang some wonderful hymns."

"Hmm. I daresay you could use some religion while you are here, Miss Madison. I do insist that you come with us to church."

Olivia tensed, exchanging glances with Sally, whose face betrayed concern for her mother's determination. Olivia wanted to inform Mrs. Hamilton she would go when she felt ready, but that would not be proper. After all, she was a guest of the house and beholden to them for their hospitality. She would respect their wishes. Why her spirit would say otherwise, she didn't know.

"I packed a picnic, Mother," Sally interrupted. "Henry wants to take me on a picnic this afternoon." Then to Olivia she added, "The men have the day off from work at the station unless there's a rescue. I'm sure Jake has the day off, too. Maybe he is free for a picnic as well?"

"I'm sure Mr. Harris has other plans," she said quickly. But it would do her good to see him. She admitted she was growing fond of him, particularly of his steadiness and forthright behavior. She could also inquire about the cargo being stored at his station. She had not even looked at it since its arrival, and she was anxious to see if any pieces had been broken or otherwise tainted by swimming in the sea-water of the hold.

Olivia helped herself to a warm muffin and drank down the delicious brew Sally said was fine coffee. Normally an ardent tea drinker, Olivia found the taste potent but good. It affected her too as if a fire had been lit in her spirit.

"It's just the coffee," Sally said with a laugh when Olivia described its effects. "It will do that to you. At the station, the men drink a lot of it to keep them awake, especially if they must work late at night. I've seen Henry up all night." She bowed her head when her mother looked at her disapprovingly. "Not that I stay with him, of course."

"I should say not!" her mother declared.

Olivia finished her muffin while pondering the upcoming excursion to church. She looked down at the ill-fitting dress, wishing she had one of the fine gowns lost at sea in the trunk she had brought from England. Dare she ask the family if they had a spare Sunday best for her to wear? She said nothing for the present as she helped carry the dishes into the kitchen and proceeded to fill the washbasin with hot water from a pot on the cookstove.

"It certainly is wonderful to see a young lady eager to help with the chores," Mrs. Hamilton observed.

"I'm happy to do a few chores here. It's the least I can do as I have no other money to help pay for my lodging." She paused, wondering about that and how long they would allow her to remain.

Mrs. Hamilton waved away her unspoken concern. "We are only glad to help. You aren't the first shipwrecked passenger I've taken in, though you are the first woman. I've had several men stay here. One stayed on as a boarder for a few weeks. I pitied them, having lost so much at sea."

"A very kind thing for you to do, Mrs. Hamilton." She smiled politely and returned to cleaning the dishes. "Also, I wonder if you might have another dress to spare for church? This one I fear doesn't fit very well. I worry I might trip on the hem."

"Goodness, look at you. I had no idea Sally's dress would be so ill-fitting. I'm not sure if I have any that will not need some alteration, but I will see what I can find."

Olivia waited patiently while Mrs. Hamilton sifted through the garments in a wardrobe and finally appeared with a dress. "Sally wore this just a few years ago before she sprouted. It may fit you better."

Olivia took the frilly dress that looked as if it were made for a young girl. She politely went to try it on, even as she wondered how to make a few coins to buy some kind of gown. Slipping into the blue frills and wide skirt, she studied it in the mirror. A least the hem didn't drag and the sleeves were the appropriate length. Mrs. Hamilton found an extra set of gloves for her to wear along with supplying an older reticule for a handkerchief. "My, that looks very nice. I'm sure Sally has a hat you could borrow, as well."

Olivia smiled as politely as she could and followed the matriarch to the sitting room, thinking she looked more like some frilled pillow one might find paired with a duvet. Sally flew into the room just then, dressed in a pleasing outfit of a long pleated skirt and formfitting blouse. She stopped short and laughed when she saw Olivia. "Mother, not that dress! I wore it to a birthday party when I was twelve!"

"Well, it fits her, and no one need know. Beggars can't be choosers. Come along, we mustn't be late."

Inwardly Olivia groaned, thankful no one would know her there. Soon this would be a memory and she would be in Raleigh among Uncle's personal friends, wearing a lovely frock he would buy for her.

She followed the two women as they strolled out of their house and into the bright October sunshine. Ocean breezes scattered the colored leaves like falling rain. The air was crisp and clear. Several villagers greeted Mrs. Hamilton and her daughter while giving Olivia looks of interest or curiosity. Despite it being Sunday the town appeared quite lively with villagers going about their business. Some even disregarded the Sabbath and carried fishing poles, outfitted in rugged gear and long boots, ready for a catch in the sound. Olivia paid no mind to the many men out on the street, all of whom gave her the once-over. Instead she thought of the delightful strolls she once took in her home country.

Her native England was far different from this sandy stretch of coast on a narrow strip of land nestled between the sound and the mighty Atlantic. In England there was plenty of lush green grass, arbors covered in ivy and roses, castle-like structures and towers made of solid stone. Here were simple houses constructed of boards, sandy ground that yielded rushes and spiked plants, the tips of which were as sharp as a sewing needle. A few trees had begun to turn with the passage of the season. The people here were different too—rough in appearance with skin weathered by the wind and sun and voices scratchy from the salty air. It was a community bound by its association with the ocean that had seen its share of triumph and tragedy. Like the dangerous shoals just off the coast that ripped apart unsuspecting ships, so too Olivia learned of violent wind storms that sometimes destroyed homes and businesses and even caused people to die. Here they struggled to survive.

Olivia forced down the emotion and followed Mrs. Hamilton and Sally into a home where the people sat on benches and chairs. The simple gathering place—in the spacious parlor of a regular house—took Olivia by surprise. She had expected some great cathedral or at least a humble church building and not this modest place of meeting. She took her seat beside Sally and folded her hands primly in her lap.

"See…that's the one who wears men's clothes," she heard a woman remark in a haughty whisper.

"She came all this way with men at her command. By herself no less," acknowledged another.

"Disgraceful."

Whispers abounded, which did not hearten Olivia to feel accepted among the villagers. She shifted in her seat and eyed the exit to the room when a man came up to them.

"It's nice to see you, Mrs. Hamilton," greeted a tall man, dressed in dark trousers and a jacket. "How is your family? I heard you went to visit them."

"They are doing well, Reverend Hall. Thank you for asking. I'd like you to meet my boarder, Miss Madison. She was shipwrecked a few days ago and was rescued by the brave men of the lifesaving station."

"So I've heard of you," the man spoke to Olivia. "You're quite famous here."

Uncertain how to take the comment, Olivia simply smiled and nodded. The reverend moved on to greet others in the tiny congregation. Just then a commotion erupted in the rear of the house. Several men entered, donned in their rough clothing and caps, which they hastily removed before taking seats in the back row. Olivia blinked as the stark gaze of Jake Harris met hers. He was accompanied by Bodie and the brash Grayson. Olivia felt warmth invade her at the thought of Jake sitting in the back, his eyes gazing at her from behind. Just then Sally turned and waved in Bodie's direction.

"Sally, mind yourself. We are in church," her

mother said with a loud whisper. "And we are about to begin."

Sally giggled and turned promptly to face front where the reverend stood behind a desk and greeted everyone present. He then asked all to rise while a woman played "How Great Thou Art" on the piano. Olivia tried to concentrate on the song and then the reverend, who spoke for a long time about the Almighty's guiding hand in matters of life. Instead she found herself distracted by the men seated in the back row. She could envision Jake sitting perfectly still, his eyes focused on the man of God, his fingers clutching the Bible. For certain he found courage and strength in listening to these words of hope. To Olivia, words from the Bible always seemed just that—mere words. She felt no life in them nor did she feel close to the Almighty. But she could hardly forget the light in Jake's eyes when he talked about God as if He were real to him and not merely a sermon or a building. Olivia had yet to understand that kind of relationship with one's Maker.

When the meeting concluded, the villagers bustled around, greeting each other. Olivia stood to one side, watching them interact, thinking how out of place she felt and wishing she was with her kin. Or better yet, with the friends back home in England whom she dearly missed. She moved quickly to the exit and stepped outside to breathe in the fresh air rather than the stale air of the crowded parlor.

Suddenly she was greeted by a man in tattered

clothing and smelling like stale tobacco smoke. His dry lips, surrounded by beard stubble, cracked into a leer. She turned and hastened down the street.

"What's yer hurry, miss?" he called.

"I'm simply taking my leave, thank you."

"Not so fast. We heard about you, you know. You may wear that fancy dress, but we hears you're the captain of a boat. The one that got caught up there in the shoals. That true?"

She stopped and whirled to face him. "I was not the captain."

"I also hear—" he paused, turned his face to one side and spat a wad of brown onto the ground "—you're a thieving gal. A pirate. Just like them stories of that lady pirate a hundred years ago. Name of Anne Bonny. It's like she's come back from the dead, she has."

"Are you filled with heavy drink? That's preposterous. Where did you hear such a lie?"

"Ah, it's no lie, miss. We run into a crew from a boat up north there near Currituck and they told us about the plundering. Some had lost their merchandise when they tried to help another boat that asked for aid. Then we hears how you took fellows under your command from the station to get the cargo off yer boat 'fore it sank. And you won't let no one near it, either. All looks mighty suspicious to me."

"And you, sir, believe tall tales and lies. The cargo is mine, carried all the way from England, given by living souls for my needs. So mind your own affairs and leave mine to me." She strode away, only to hear footsteps behind. Her pace quickened. The rascal now followed her; the memory of his foul breath and blood-tinged eyes branded in her mind. From the tension at the lifesaving station, to the losses endured, and now this wicked claim with no merit whatsoever, she only wanted a refuge from the storms of life. The reverend had spoken of such things, of refuge and peace, as if the words were meant for her. But there was nothing like that anywhere. *Dear God, why?*

The footsteps continued until at last she turned. Jake was hurrying after her. "What's the matter? Why are you running? I wanted to say hello back at the house but…"

She brushed back a lock of hair that had fallen out of the chignon and breathed a sigh of relief. "I—I was frightened," she managed to say.

"I'm sorry. I didn't mean to frighten you." He paused. "You look as though you've had a shock. Are you all right?"

No! Far from it! she thought in despair. *I feel weak when I should feel strong and secure. I should be in my uncle's stead, at peace. Instead I'm stranded here until word arrives, and he comes for me. I am beholden to a lovesick young girl and her headstrong mother. And everyone in this village thinks I am strange or manly or even a pirate named Bonny, of all things!* She wished with all her might she could voice these burdens to Jake. But he too seemed to have his own personal difficulties. No one was her advocate in this place. No one understood. "I'm fine," she now declared, inhaling a deep breath. "Thank you for your concern. Now I must go."

"No, you're not fine. You look troubled, and I haven't helped matters or been understanding. I came to apologize for what I said yesterday."

"I bear no grudge, Mr. Harris. It isn't you, in all honesty. I only wish..." She hesitated. "I wish we hadn't shipwrecked. I wish the brave men and my maid hadn't perished." Her voice choked. "God abandoned me in my time of need. I don't understand this or why long-suffering souls continue to suffer."

Jake stepped forward, his face softening under the glow of the sun's rays. Olivia caught her breath, thinking then how handsome he really was.

"Even if we don't understand why, God hasn't abandoned us. You heard the sermon today. He cares for us. Look at what He has already done for you. You were safely rescued. You have your cargo. You have a fine place to stay with women who care about you."

"I suppose. Now if only I had a decent dress to wear." She chuckled. "Oh, I shouldn't complain. Like you said, the people here have come to my aid, and I'm grateful, even if I fail at times to show it. It's just that I feel out of place, like a ship wandering at sea without a place to weigh anchor."

"I don't understand why you are worried about a dress, seeing as you prefer men's clothing?"

Her face colored. "I never prefer men's attire, Mr.

Harris. I wore men's garments only out of necessity while on the ship. I was quite the lady in my native country, thank you."

"Of course. I apologize. But you needn't worry. Your uncle will come for you soon, I'm sure. Did you send word of your condition?"

"The letter will post tomorrow. Maybe I should have tried to reach him by telegraph."

"You will hear soon."

He sounded so convincing, Olivia dearly wished she could cling to his confidence rather than dwell on the weight of her doubt. Maybe this was what Jake meant by faith in the midst of trials. How difficult it was to grab hold despite the raging tempest, like the day the ship faced the fierce storm in the Atlantic. Sometimes it takes faith just to have faith.

Now she managed to bring her thoughts about to their current situation. She asked Jake if he had heard any news of the board member's arrival.

"We don't know yet when he will come. Tomorrow, bright and early, we need to clean the station from top to bottom. Shine whatever can be shined and make sure the equipment is in good working order."

"Well, I'll be glad to tell whoever arrives at your station of your efforts the night of my rescue. It's the least I can do."

"Thank you."

She paused, thinking on the accusation brought forth by the grizzly man who confronted her on the street. "Jake, I must ask something else. Have you heard any rumors of late?"

"Rumors of what?"

"Like piracy in these parts?"

He cast her a strange look for only a moment then shook his head. "Not of active piracy off the coast. There is always some scoundrel trying to steal something, of course. But piracy in this region is mostly from legends passed down. Like Blackbeard for instance. Back in the 1700s, he was the most notorious pirate to sail the seven seas. They say his hideout was in some cove near Ocracoke Island." He paused. "Why do you ask?"

"Just that I heard something of it. I remember also the British crown was involved in dealing with pirates that plundered the trade routes. On occasion my father had to deal with it." Her voice faded away.

"Well, there's no reason for concern if you're worried about your cargo. I've been keeping watch at the storehouse."

"Thank you. I appreciate it very much." The news brought some measure of relief to an otherwise troubled heart. Maybe there was goodness to be found within the hearts of others, like Jacob Harris. If nothing else, she could thank the Lord of heaven that Jake had brought her to safety and now kept watch over the things that concerned her. Maybe he was sent as a shining light in a dark time. If only he would remain that way and not be snuffed out as many other shining lights had been in her life.

Chapter 9

Olivia paced about the sitting room, glancing at the large oak outside the window, now turning a rustic sienna color with the coming autumn. Ten days had gone by since the letter was sent and still no word from her uncle. What would she do if she didn't hear from him or if, heaven forbid, something had happened? Where would she go? She considered it as she paced, her mind a jumble of thoughts.

As time passed, she felt increasingly beholden to Mrs. Hamilton and her daughter for her stay here. The lack of money to pay for her lodgings weighed heavily on her. She tried helping around the house but with Georgiana there earning money by also doing chores and cooking, Olivia felt she was becoming a burden. She must also do something soon about the cargo stored at the lifesaving station. Each day she grew more anxious for its safety. If her uncle did not come soon, she would need to hire someone to help her transport the goods to the mainland. She would also need to locate a reputable buyer. But before all that, she would need something of value just to help pay the expenses. Perhaps she could open one small crate and try to barter with the general store in Hatteras Village.

"What's troubling you, Olivia?" a voice inquired.

Olivia turned to see Sally standing in the doorway with a wicker basket over one arm, dressed in a cape and hat as if ready for an excursion. No doubt she was taking a walk with her beau, who came calling nearly every noon hour. "Just praying that my uncle writes me soon."

"It takes time to send word from here to the mainland and vice versa. You will hear soon, I'm sure."

Olivia smiled at the young woman's optimism, hoping it would lift her own spirits. Some days she would walk among the dunes, gazing at the lifesaving station beyond a few of the humble dwellings and think about Jake. Why him of all men? He had words of wisdom, to be sure. He possessed a fine Christian nature. How far she felt from godly things though, and especially the way he thought of things. She had never considered it until now. Christianity to her had always been simply a religion, not a life that one lived and breathed. Jacob Harris lived it like no one she had ever met. And she was beginning to fall in love with its truthfulness and purpose, its freedom and its peace…and maybe with the man too, though she couldn't be certain of anything.

Olivia felt a hand on her arm and looked back to find Sally still there. "Come with me," Sally coaxed. "I'm going to the ladies' sewing circle. You can meet the others."

"I'm afraid I won't be much help. I don't sew." After the encounter with the grizzled man on the street, Olivia had been avoiding the public altogether these days.

"I'll teach you. It will give you something to do rather than pining away here."

Olivia shook her head. "I've been meaning to remedy that. I should be paying for my stay and your kindness. I don't know how much longer it will be before Uncle receives word. Is there a place where I can conduct a trade?"

"You mean like to sell goods? We have a trader who comes every so often from the mainland. Mr. Sumners will be here Friday. He usually sells, but he will likely buy, too."

"That sounds perfect. Does he sell dress goods?"

"He sells all kinds of goods. I do love it when he comes. I never know what he will have. Sometimes it's gloves or a hat." She lowered her voice. "Mother has a fit over the money I spend."

Olivia managed a smile, but all she could think of was how this might be the answer to her money troubles. "Well, it would be interesting to look. If he is willing to trade, all the better."

"I'm sure he will help you. And if you need any suggestions for fashion, just ask. Now come learn some sewing. I've told the ladies about you. All of them are eager to meet you."

Olivia would rather brave another stormy sea than be in the company of unpredictable women, but she was in Sally's debt. Perhaps learning a skill like sewing might be useful one day. Maybe she will have shirts to sew for her husband and children. Just the thought made her feel warm. There had only been the lords of England who could well afford some waif to sew their clothing. They desired women of noble means. She was no longer in noble England but here in the rustic United States where men and women labored hard by the ocean to keep their meager lifestyle. There were no fancy manor homes or large land holdings like England. Here there were modest dwellings nestled beside the roar of the ocean and the odor of the sea, with rugged men in boats, laboring to bring in the day's catch. And yes, there were also the rugged men of the lifesaving station who rescued lost souls from the deep. Like Jake.

Olivia accepted an apron from Sally along with a cape and hat as the day was brisk. A cold wind blew up from the ocean, bringing with it a dampness and perhaps the hint of rain to come. They hurried along the humble street of Hatteras Village. Those they met were engaged in their daily activities. Olivia considered what she might be doing on a day like today back in England. Doing as Sally said, most likely.

Pining away for nothing in particular. Worrying over her future and the future of her brother. "Dearest Nathan, I pray you are well," she murmured.

"What was that?"

"I was thinking about my brother back in England. I wonder when I will see him again."

Sally nodded. "I'm an only child, so I never had to worry about a brother or sister. I used to ask my mother why I was alone. She said I was enough, even though she did lose several other babies. She often said I was worth more than ten children."

Olivia smiled. "What could she mean you were enough? You seem so saintly in your ways."

"It wasn't in the manner of disobedience. She meant that I was all she needed to feel content."

Olivia wanted to ask where her father was but thought it too prying. "Mr. Harris told me he had lost a brother."

"Henry said something about that. Now Jake thinks of Henry as a brother."

"Do you know what happened?"

"Jake's true brother drowned in a boating accident."

Olivia drew in a sharp breath. "How awful."

"That's why he went into lifesaving. He refused to have the ocean take another life if he could help it. Henry told me the story. There aren't many secrets I don't know."

Olivia's heart warmed all the more at the thought of Jake and the sorrows he bore, much like her own. But more importantly, he used the loss as a means to save others. "He's an incredible man," she said softly.

"I thought there might be something between you. Henry says Jake is really taken."

Olivia drew the cape tighter around her shoulders. "Oh?"

"He talks about you all the time. I mean, I don't think of a rescue as some romantic endeavor, but once a man saves you…it can't help but change hearts."

Olivia felt the heat build in her face. "H-he was only doing his duty that night."

Sally laughed again and stopped before a modest home. "Here we are. Come, I'll introduce you."

Olivia followed her in to greet the other four women gathered in a small room, all with baskets of notions resting at their feet and embroidery hoops in their hands. "May I introduce Olivia Madison, who is a guest in our home."

"You're the one who was shipwrecked!" one of the girls announced.

Olivia wondered if this was common knowledge in the village. Likely they didn't get too many shipwrecked women staying in their humble hamlet. "I'm thankful for the lifesaving station here. Without the brave men who risked their lives to save my own, I would not have survived."

"The men do work hard," said another woman whom Sally introduced as the matron of the sewing circle, Mrs. Lears. "When there is a rescue, that is.

But I fear at times they can become too interested in drink and carousing."

"Only when they are bored," said another young woman Sally introduced as Margot. "I hear they are quite busy from what one of the surfmen told me. They are expecting a visit from a government official any day now. So they have been on their best behavior, working to make the station bright and tidy."

Mrs. Lears nodded. "Very nice. Perhaps I will bake them some pies after all."

The women bent over their sewing, sharing in other town gossip. Sally withdrew her embroidery to show Olivia. She looked at the intricate work of the sampler, the delicate stitches that formed a row of the old English alphabet and shook her head when Sally offered to show her how to stitch. Her clumsy fingers had only known toil and labor for these many months. They could never handle a needle and thread. Olivia was content to sit in their company, observe, and be a curiosity for others.

"Can you tell us how it was you were shipwrecked?" asked Margot. "I have lived here all my life and don't ever recall meeting a woman survivor living in Hatteras."

"I came here from England on family business, looking to see my uncle in Raleigh. We were nearly to port when the storm blew us off course."

"Dear me, that's how it is," said Mrs. Lears before biting off the blue thread. "Those hapless young captains don't understand the dangerous waters here. Their pride makes them believe they can conquer anything. Then a sudden wind drives them too close to the Diamond Shoals where they shipwreck. So it is."

The women nodded in agreement. Olivia sat there feeling condemned, as if she or the crew had done something terribly wrong. "There is only so much one can do when a tempest brews at sea," she finally said. "Have any of you been in a storm at sea?"

They looked up briefly then returned to their sewing. No one spoke a word.

"Even the best sailor cannot move a ship in a tug-of-war with the waves. Only God can move it."

"You are very right, my dear," said Mrs. Lears. "Obviously God desired to have you here in our village for a reason."

"I hardly know whatever for," Olivia confessed.

The woman smiled knowingly. "I'm sure in time you will come to know the reason why."

Olivia continued to sit with her hands folded while the conversation muted to a discomforting silence and the women gave her cautious glances. That was, until Margot asked about the baby grandson born to Mrs. Wilson, and they all began chirping on that subject. After about fifteen more minutes of gossip, Mrs. Lears stood to fetch the tea.

"I think I will take my leave now," Olivia told Sally in a low voice. "I need to see about the cargo and find out what I can have ready for the trader when he comes to the village."

"Are you sure you want to leave now? Mrs. Lears makes the most delicious desserts."

Olivia chose not to reveal her true feelings—that in this circle she felt more like an object of conversation found in a store window than a person of value. "I'm quite certain. Thank you for inviting me." Olivia stood, smiled her thanks to the small group and headed for the door.

"Leaving us so soon?" Mrs. Lears inquired. Her hands clasped a tea tray containing slices of chocolate cake on small rosebud plates.

The cake did look delicious, but Olivia still edged her way to the door. "Yes. I—I have some matters to look after. But thank you for your hospitality and kind words."

"I do mean what I say. You may not know why you are here, but God does. And He cares about that…and about you."

Olivia managed a small smile and ventured out into the blustery October day, even as the tears stung her eyes. *She may be right, but God has yet to confide in me about it. Or about anything else in my life, for that matter.*

Jake and the other surfmen worked diligently with the signal flags that warned ships of danger as well as receiving communications from ships in distress. When Jake first became a surfman, it took him some time to understand all that was required in this position. From learning the beach apparatus drill to the upkeep of the station to using the signal flags, each skill must be practiced until perfected. Especially now with the pending arrival of the lifesaving board member who had been inexplicably delayed. But today Jake was not without his distraction, mainly in the form of Olivia Madison. He thought of the meeting in church for many days thereafter. Removed from the men's clothing she'd worn on the day they'd rescued the cargo, she looked beautiful in a blue dress and bustle that accentuated her feminine form. Jake could hardly believe she had journeyed across the ocean with men at her command. She could have been any of the women walking the streets of Hatteras Village, if not for the authoritative attitude that permeated her being.

All had been quiet as far as any lifesaving activity since the day of Olivia's rescue at sea. Not long after the final rescue of the ship's cargo, a brief burst of wind ultimately dealt the final blow to the schooner's remains, committing it to a salty grave. At times the remains of Olivia's ship would wash ashore in the form of splintered boards, all fragments of a once proud and able-bodied vessel that carried souls across the Atlantic. Now it was only good as tinder to feed a bonfire. For some strange reason, it saddened him.

Jake returned to the station to see the men gathered around the coffeepot. He took a cup of the potent brew and decided to take another beach patrol walk with Bodie. Bodie's young face was distraught when he talked about the surfman John.

"He refused to do the patrol correctly, Jake. And then when he made it to the next station, he took off on his own. I didn't see him for the rest of the evening. If there had been a distress call last night..."

The mere fact angered Jake. Lives might have been lost because of John's recklessness. But after his ill-fated confrontation, there was little Jake could do. "Just be sure you are doing your part and leave him to God. In due time he will reap what he sows."

"He ought to at least sow a lower rank," Bodie noted with a sniff. "When do you think I'll stop being surfman number six?"

"When the keeper has seen what you can do without complaint."

Bodie nodded. He then said something Jake hadn't expected. "Do you miss Olivia Madison's company?"

"Do I miss Olivia Madison's company?" he repeated. His heart leaped. Of course he missed her, but he didn't dare say so. He missed everything about her. The beauty of her chiseled face. Her smile. The fine English accent that gave a delightful lilt to her words. Her adventuresome ways, even when they sometimes infuriated him. But she was only here until her uncle came and whisked her away. After the embarrassing aftermath with his first love, Jake dared not open his heart to another, especially one with a different destiny than his own. He'd learned an important lesson from that incident and refused to fall in love with the wrong woman. For him, love was like a shipwreck, bound only to be dragged and destroyed on the Diamond Shoals of fate. He would do better to leave romance to others and concentrate on his duty.

"You look like you're on another island," Grayson commented, coming up to them, holding a cup of coffee that blew steam into his face.

"He misses the company of Olivia Madison," Bodie said with a smile.

Jake felt the heat enter his face and quickly decided to change the topic of conversation. "So what are you doing on the last week before the official season begins, Grayson?"

"I'm not taking leave. As the lead surfman, the keeper wishes me to learn the duties of the station. I think we may soon be having a change of leadership, which could be the reason an official is paying us a visit."

Jake straightened. "I had no idea the keeper was leaving."

"I don't think I'm ready to take over the reins of this station, either."

"Of course you are, Grayson. You were born to it. You know it better than anyone. Every surfman here trusts you."

Grayson sighed. "Unfortunately we no longer

work together. Ever since that day we rescued the English damsel in distress, I feel we are fractured. The sooner she is picked up by her uncle and leaves here, the better it will be."

Jake blinked, wondering what prompted Grayson's accusatory tone toward Olivia Madison. "Surely Miss Madison isn't to blame for the division among us. Our own pride and foolishness does that well enough."

"Six unmarried men and a woman who appears to visit more often than is needed, and with her cargo stored in our storehouse—it can't help but cause a disruption to our activity."

Just then Jake caught sight of a figure with the wind sweeping her gown, heading in the direction of the station.

"And speaking of Miss Madison..." Bodie said. "Here comes the lady of the sea."

Jake hurriedly drank down his coffee. He felt his heart race as Olivia Madison drew near. Was it God's doing or was she simply distracting him, as Grayson surmised?

"Jake, go see what she wants and be done with it," Grayson said. "Then you must direct your attention to your duties."

Jake put down the cup and left, walking briskly across the sandy ground. "Good day, Miss Madison. What can we do for you?"

"I am here to see about my cargo."

"Have you heard from your uncle? Are you ready

to depart?" His voice wavered with those last words. He realized at that moment he didn't want her to leave, despite what Grayson said. The sensation had never been as great as it was now.

She laughed. "Ah, so eager to have me on my way. I'm certain you aren't the only one. Anyway, I plan to leave just as soon as the arrangements can be made. But for now, I'm short of money. The cargo is my only source of income."

Jake found her statement curious. *What exactly do those crates contain?* he wondered. "Do you need help? I have a small amount of money and will gladly..."

"All I have need of is right here. But I could use a jimmy, if you please." She hesitated. "And I would prefer this not be a sideshow, you understand. I need to retrieve what is required on my own accord and without prying eyes into a person's affairs."

Jake stiffened. Why did she have to be as cold as the icy waters of the north Atlantic? What happened to the woman he'd met on the street? The one who desperately sought peace and protection? "The men are inside the station. It will be mealtime soon. No one will bother you."

"Good. I prefer it that way, thank you." She hesitated. "You have been good to me since my arrival here, Mr. Harris. I wish we hadn't exchanged such harsh words in the past, but they were likely born from uncertainty in our circumstances, don't you think?"

"Uncertainty?" he repeated. "I'm not sure what you mean. But I think it's better for everyone if you are safe at home with relatives rather than in this strange place. Each of us goes through things that burden us. I would say it's the cares of this world that can force us to say and do things we sometimes regret."

"That makes sense." She sighed. "And now the jimmy, if you please?"

"I'll be right back." He scurried away, noticing John out of the corner of his eye but thinking little of it as he concentrated on fulfilling Olivia's request.

Chapter 10

Jake did as Olivia asked and left her alone while she pried open a crate to examine the contents. She selected a few items to stow in a large sack then asked for a hammer to nail the crate back up. He wondered about her secrecy and why she defended her possessions to the last. The goods she claimed were to save a life. Yet she acted as if she were concealing some other plan as well, though he couldn't imagine what.

She hefted the bag over her shoulder. "Thank you for your help, Mr. Harris. It means a great deal. I won't take up any more of your time." She turned to walk away.

"Why are you being so secretive about what your ship carried?"

She whirled at his pointed question that came out quicker than he anticipated. "It… This cargo is invaluable to me. Many have worked hard and even sacrificed their lives for it. I won't see it jeopardized by possible thievery."

"Don't you trust me?" The connotation behind her words had hurt worse than if they'd been uttered by anyone else. But the fact was plain: she didn't trust him. She thought of him and the others as miscreants. Though right now, what did it matter? She would soon be on her way, carrying her valuables with her. She would disappear, never to be heard from again. A sinking feeling filled his heart.

When she didn't answer him further, Jake turned and left. He entered the station to find a meal of fish chowder and baking powder biscuits as hard as nails. Jake took his place at the long table, noticing at once that all eyes seemed to be on him. It made him feel warm, wondering why the others were looking at him so strangely. Unless they had seen him and Olivia together and felt some mischief were afoot. Jake swallowed, not wishing to make himself a further spectacle, considering what had happened on the beach with the Lyle gun during the drill. As it was, John still sported the faint outline of a bruise on his cheek, though this night he wore a wry grin that left Jake feeling uneasy.

Grayson stood at the head of the table and offered the grace for the meal. When he sat down, the others followed suit. No one uttered a word. Spoons clinked against bowls and mouths were stuffed with crumbling biscuits. Again Jake caught the looks given by the men. Even Bodie stared at him strangely. He tensed.

"I believe the training went well today," Grayson finally declared. "We seem to have the signal flags down well. Tomorrow is more practice with the beach apparatus drill. And I have it in confidence that the member of the board should arrive by Friday to witness our operations."

"We're gonna be in trouble for sure then," John mumbled.

"What was that, John?" Grayson asked.

"Only that we've got trouble brewing here at the station and no one knows about it. But if we don't take care of it, we're gonna find ourselves in deep water, especially with the board member coming. It could be enough to sink this lifesaving station, and I know it." He eyed Jake. "And Jake here knows exactly what I'm talking about, don't you, Jake?"

Jake tensed even further, realizing his fears were coming true. The men thought he had engaged in some inappropriate contact with Olivia Madison. He opened his mouth to counter the accusation when Grayson interrupted him.

"What exactly do you mean?" Grayson asked.

"There are rumors all over the village that his lady of the sea is involved in piracy. And I have a letter that proves it."

All at once spoons fell into their bowls with loud

clinks. Every eye was fixed on John, and the men's mouths hung open in astonishment.

Jake flew to his feet. "That is absurd!"

"I expected as much from you," John snarled. "You were out there aiding in her theft just today. I saw you help get the goods with a jimmy, acting just like an accomplice."

Jake felt his face redden with the building heat inside him. "What are you saying? The crates contain Miss Madison's possessions. They are to help free her brother who was falsely arrested in England. Only now she needs them for money as she is penniless." He stood firm until he recalled Olivia's statement after church many days ago—that she had heard rumors of piracy. And just today he observed her aloofness with her cargo. The strong arm of doubt now tried to invade him as it swept around the table.

"Do you really believe some tale of a long-lost brother?" John pushed himself back from his place and whisked a crumpled paper out of his pocket. "I see you haven't heard the news. Or any of you." He waved the paper before them. "I got this from a fellow working the north station up there in Currituck. It seems a boat they helped rescue a few weeks ago had been boarded on the high seas and the goods stripped. They said it was armed pirates. And there was a woman on board in some position of leadership. They'd never seen that before except in legends. Now it's happened." He thrust the paper toward Grayson. "See for yourself."

Grayson took the paper to examine it, even as Jake felt every nerve stand on edge.

"This is an official notification to the other stations concerning possible acts of piracy," Grayson acknowledged gravely. "We are to report any unusual activity to the authorities." He cleared his throat and read it aloud.

> "Currituck Station, October 12, 1881. We have been alerted to recent reports of piracy off the Atlantic seaboard. A vessel rescued by the station had been plundered and its cargo seized by a small schooner bearing no markings, rumored to be commanded by a female captain. All stations are to report any unusual activity, along with any inquiries or questions, to the lifesaving board and to the local authorities."

"See? It says to be on the lookout for a woman captain." John's stark gray eyes settled once more on Jake. "So what did that woman have in the cargo anyway, Jake? You were there. Tell us. It might give a clue as to where she got it."

He thought of Olivia's preoccupation with the cargo, her demand to have it guarded and, the most peculiar thing of all, her insistence he not see any of it. "I don't know. She wouldn't let me look at it."

The men murmured and shook their heads. Grayson folded the paper and sat down. "I'm sure the keeper is aware of this already, but I will bring it to his attention. However, we are not to jump to any conclusions without proof."

"We have the proof right under our noses!" John declared. "I say we take charge of the cargo and inspect it ourselves."

"We have no right to commandeer cargo without just cause," Jake said. "As it is, you have been prying into Miss Madison's affairs from the beginning. What right have you to do any of this, surfman number four?"

"I have all the right to safeguard this station and the souls we serve. Unlike you, I wish to see the rogues brought to justice and not allow a woman to take advantage of others and get away with stealing. I tell you now, she's a pirate. She fits the description."

"I will show the keeper the letter and let him deal with this," Grayson interjected. "I suggest you put the matter aside and eat something."

Jake, however, could not eat. His mind was numb. Surely this could not be happening. It must all be just a strange coincidence. At the conclusion of the meal, he saw the damaging letter lying at Grayson's place. He took it up and reread a sentence. "A vessel rescued by the station had been plundered and its cargo seized by a small schooner bearing no markings, rumored to be commanded by a female captain."

Jake shook his head. Many ships carried cargo. Many had been caught in the breakers up north or in the Diamond Shoals near Hatteras. It's true he had never met anyone like Olivia, who willingly took the reins of leadership on a vessel. But that should not condemn her to being found guilty of some act of piracy. He nearly crushed the paper under the weight of his anger but instead put it back on the table. John was doing all this to spite him, further tarnishing his reputation before his fellow surfmen. He was looking to see Jake cast out of here for some unknown reason. But Jake refused to be moved or allow Olivia to be judged. She was no more a pirate that he. The truth was, she had suffered loss. She was doing what she felt was in her best interests, alone in this strange place. He would help one in need and not turn his back on account of some erroneous rumor, even if the odds were against him. God was using this field of trial for some great purpose, and he would hold his head high until the bitter end.

But for now his thoughts were interrupted when Grayson asked if he would take Bodie on the nightly beach patrol. Jake was glad to do it and rid himself of what had occurred this night. He found the lantern and Coston signals and joined Bodie. The young man appeared strangely quiet, without his usual exuberance for the venture. Only when they had walked the beach for a time did Jake finally ask what was bothering him.

"I'm worried about the news John shared," he said. "If that woman is a pirate, there's no telling what she could do. And she's staying with my Sally and her mother. Even now she might be stealing from them! I—I need to warn them."

Jake stopped in his tracks and whirled to face the man. He held the lantern high in the air, allowing the glow to reflect off Bodie's concerned face. "You'll do no such thing. This is a scheme perpetrated by John. You know it."

"I might have believed you until I saw the letter. You did, too. Did he make that up? I hardly think so."

"It doesn't mean Olivia is a pirate. Or the pirate of Currituck for that matter. The notion is ludicrous. It's wrong to accuse without facts."

Bodie shook his head. "I'm not so sure about that, Jake. You must admit that Miss Madison has been acting peculiar ever since she arrived here. Her thoughts day and night are on her cargo. Maybe she does possess things of value, like loot from other ships. Maybe that's why she is so protective of the cargo, for fear of being found out." He tensed. "If so, I can't have her living anymore with my Sally. It's too dangerous."

"Bodie, there's no reason to think ill of her. What if someone accused you of stealing because you possessed a coat similar to the one that went missing? Would you think it just?"

Bodie stayed silent. Jake knew they needed to be watching the ocean for ships in trouble and not creating their own troubles on the beach. But he sensed everything slipping away if he did not put a stop to it. Perhaps he needed to settle the question once and for all and confront Olivia outright. Demand that he see her cargo and proof of ownership, though he knew what her reaction would be. If he didn't intervene and soon, it would not only be her integrity put into question but his, too.

The incident was suddenly thrust aside when Jake caught sight of a white glow soaring into the air. All things disappeared when a ship signaled distress. He jumped into action, handing off the lantern to Bodie while he lit a return signal. He never thought he would be glad for a rescue, but tonight he was. For the rest of the evening he and the others worked together as a lifesaving station should, helping save an imperiled crew.

When the tasks were completed later that evening, the keeper called Grayson, Jake and Bodie for a meeting before they retired for the night.

"Why does he want to see us now?" Jake asked Grayson.

Grayson said nothing. Entering the office, the keeper greeted them with a grim expression, placing his hands on his desk.

"I've heard the rumors of the piracy," the keeper said, "and that it may involve the passenger we rescued a few weeks ago. However, until we have proof of the matter, there will be no further discussion of this among the men. I have already spoken to surfman number four about it."

"But what about the safety of my girl?" Bodie asked. "That woman lives with her and her mother. What if she is planning some mischief?"

"Bodie, you know as well as I that will not happen," Jake interrupted.

The keeper raised his voice. "As I said, we will take up this matter when further proof is available. But for now it is to be treated as a rumor only. On Friday the board member arrives to inspect the station. We must show we are a strong and vital station here on the cape if we are to survive. And that means excellence in every respect and working together. There will be no further talk of this. That is all."

Jake was grateful at least to see the keeper siding with him on the matter. Maybe he had Grayson to thank for it. Grayson was not abandoning their friendship but believed in the truth. When the men moved off to retire for the night, he met Grayson in the foyer as he was saying good-night to the keeper. "Thank you, Grayson. I know you spoke to the keeper about this. I appreciate it."

"We all worked hard tonight with the rescue. I'm glad to see that even with everything we've been through in the past week, we can still come together as one for the common good."

"Actually, I meant for coming on the side of Olivia's interests."

Grayson stared at him. "I only informed the keeper of what was happening among the men. We can't have any distractions right now. We need to let this alone and concentrate on our duties."

"You don't believe the rumors about Olivia, do you?"

"I believe the letter John showed us to be factual.

But as to Miss Madison's involvement, I have no way of knowing. I suppose if she is willing to reveal her cargo and prove her innocence, the matter can be put to rest. I'm sure she will want to clear her name."

Jake frowned. "Why must the innocent be forced to clear their name before rogues like John?"

"Even our Lord and Master knows what it is like to be condemned, even to die, despite His innocence," Grayson reminded him. "Trust that God will help Miss Madison overcome this as the Almighty has in other matters of her life. Keep to what is important—the board's visit and this station—and leave the rest in God's hands."

Leave the rest in God's hands. It proved difficult to do when every part of him screamed to jump into action like surfmen did in times of need. When the men had assembled in the bunkroom for the night, Jake grabbed his coat and slipped out of the station. The sandy beach glowed in the pale light of the rising moon. He turned to see the storehouse in the distance where Olivia's cargo was kept. He thought of the jimmy and wondered if he should take it upon himself to see the evidence. But then he remembered his disdain over John invading Olivia's personal property by reading her journal. No, he must convince Olivia to make good her name. She would help not only herself but him, as well.

He sighed. Once again the circumstances of life were in need of a rescue.

Chapter 11

Olivia wanted to wish the ill feelings away but could not. She sat inside the small room Sally and her mother allowed her to use, examining the items she managed to secure from a crate inside the storage area.

She fingered an exquisite piece of fine pearls and wondered who might have given them to use on behalf of her brother. She fastened the beaded necklace about her throat, stood and walked over to the mirror to admire it. The piece did wonders to brighten her otherwise dreary dress and sad disposition. She hoped it would fetch a fair price with the trader who would be arriving in the village.

She glanced back at the other items—a modest brass fixture and a plate painted with the intricate design of windmills, probably from Holland. She glowed then with the thought of the kind people who had given their earthly treasures to see her loved one set free. It helped ease her misgivings this day, though she didn't know why she felt uneasy. If only Uncle Dwight would contact her. Surely he must have received her letter by now. Raleigh was in the same state as this coastline according to a map she had seen in O'Malley's possession. It should take but a matter of a few days to receive the letter and then come fetch her. Maybe by Sunday he will have come and, she hoped, with a wagon large enough to haul away all this excellent cargo.

Olivia undid the strand of pearls, watching them reflect the sunlight in the palm of her hand. She fingered each pearl, wishing now she had taken something else to trade rather than this lovely strand. She wished she had the money to own it then quickly chastised herself for her covetousness. They were not her objects but Nathan's. Dear Nathan, languishing inside that cramped place, stuffed with others in tiny rooms of the debtor's prison that could not be any better than the stinking hold where the cargo had been stored. He must be miserable, calling for a rescue of his own, wondering if anyone cared. She closed her hand around the pearls. She wanted him to know that she cared. Deeply. She had journeyed all the way here, facing storm and peril, seeking a solution. And she would not rest until he was set free.

Olivia was wrapping the pretty jewelry in a piece

of cloth when she looked up to find the door to her room ajar and a set of eyes staring at her from the hall. Quickly she hid the pieces and came to the door. "Hello, Sally."

"Mother wants to see you right away," came a muffled voice.

Olivia opened the door wider to see the young woman standing there without the usual smile or excitement in her voice. She looked as if something troubled her soul. "Are you quite well?"

Sally said nothing but only motioned for her to follow. Olivia hastened down the hall and to the sitting room where Mrs. Hamilton sat embroidering. "Oh, Miss Madison. Do take a seat."

Olivia did so. "I hope I am not burdening you by staying here so long without compensation," she began. "I'm certain Uncle will come soon and…"

Mrs. Hamilton laid the hoop on her lap. "That is why I wanted to speak to you. You must seek different lodgings immediately."

Olivia sat back, stunned. "Madam, believe me, I will soon have money…"

"Oh, I don't want to cast a woman into the street," Mrs. Hamilton moaned. She stood quickly and began to pace. She threw up her hands. "But what am I to do?"

"Please. I have goods I can trade tomorrow to help pay for…"

She whirled, her eyes blazing. "No! I don't want that kind of money. I will not have you trading stolen goods to pay for your lodging. Do you understand what such money will do to me? I could be cast into jail!"

Olivia felt her jaw slip wide-open and fought to close it. What in the world was she saying? "I—I don't understand."

"Well, I do. So please gather your things and leave as quickly as you can." Mrs. Hamilton hurried out of the room.

Olivia sat stiff in the chair, paralyzed by this news. What could have possibly happened that led Mrs. Hamilton to believe the items she possessed were stolen? How could she think her a thief? She had taken nothing of value from their home or anywhere else. She would swear on her father's grave. "Mrs. Hamilton, please," she said, hurrying to the kitchen where Georgiana stood at the table, kneading dough. "Do you know where Mrs. Hamilton went?"

"No, miss. But she is rather unstrung, I must say."

"Do you know… Have you heard anything? She has asked me to leave."

Georgiana shrugged. "I am no gossip."

"I know, but…" Olivia fought back the tears that tried to make an inopportune entrance. "I was only hoping you might know the reason why. I don't mean to pry."

"It's just as Mother said," came a steely reply. Sally had entered the kitchen, her arms folded. "Leave us, Georgiana."

She curtsied and disappeared outside.

"You've been asked to leave because we can't have a thief and a liar living under our roof."

"I am not a thief!" Olivia cried. "I have taken nothing that doesn't belong to me. I have accepted your charity, yes, but only because I had nothing to my name after the storm. Please tell me why I am being accused."

"Henry was right. You are a better storyteller than old Mrs. Grimes."

Henry? She meant Bodie, Jake's friend. What did he have to do with this? What could have transpired that led him to contrive some falsehood and speak it to Sally? "I have said or done nothing to your Henry."

"He heard it at the lifesaving station. There's even a paper that proves you're a pirate. At first I didn't want to believe him. But more and more I think it might be true. You've been mysterious ever since you came here. You don't know sewing. You wear men's clothing. You're different. And maybe that difference is a sign of trouble." Sally edged toward the table and quickly picked up a knife. "I don't know if you're a pirate or not, but I will protect my mother and our home if I have to. Now please leave at once."

Olivia felt all the blood rush out of her. She became dizzy and nearly fainted as she numbly went to her room to take off the dress and return to the men's shirt and trousers she'd worn when she'd first arrived. Glancing out the window, she saw Georgiana and Mrs. Hamilton conversing in the garden. If there was only a bit of sanity left…perhaps she might find it in the older woman. When she finished dressing, she cautiously approached the garden. Georgiana hurried away with Mrs. Hamilton ready to follow suit.

"Please, madam, just a word," Olivia began. "I—I have been falsely accused. I have done nothing. I am not here to hurt you or anyone. I only want to save my brother and…"

"Please, no more. We have been kind to you, young woman, but we can do no more. Please just let us alone. We don't want to be involved in any of this." With that she scurried into the house and bolted the door shut.

No, no. And just as I was beginning to believe, to have the faith that Jake talked about. Why has God abandoned me once again? Just then she realized she had left the precious pieces of cargo in the room—the pearl necklace, the plate and the brass fixture. She had nothing but the clothing on her back, maybe not even the cargo if others at the station thought her some deviant woman with stolen property in her possession.

Walking the street in a daze, she remembered the grizzly old fisherman she had crossed paths with in the village after the church service and the conversation she had put out of her mind until now.

Not so fast. We heard about you, you know. You

may wear that fancy dress, but we hears you're the captain of a boat. The one that got caught up there in the shoals. That true?

I was not the captain, she had refuted.

I also hear you're a thieving gal. A pirate. Just like them stories of that lady pirate a hundred years ago. Name of Anne Bonny. It's like she's come back from the dead, she has.

Her soul now cried in despair. *Why am I being accused of such things? Why must I only have enemies and no friends? What have I done to deserve any of this?*

Olivia continued walking though she had no idea where to go or what to do. Everything had been denied her because of false rumors. If only she could find the ones responsible and set things right. But even if she were to confess, who would believe her?

Olivia turned away from the village and the people and everything wrong with life and walked to the shore. She watched the waves crash onto the beach and wished they played a soothing melody to her heart rather than stirring up regret and despair. She collapsed into the sand and sat there until the tide started to come in. Sea water began inching closer as the evening shadows began to descend, but she didn't care. She had no place to go and no one who cared. For the first time, she wished she had died at sea.

"Bodie, how could you do such a thing?" Jake cried when he heard the news of Olivia's departure from Sally's home. "I asked you not to jump to conclusions without proof. Even the keeper said not to. Now Olivia is out in the cold tonight with nowhere to go?"

Bodie said nothing. Jake grabbed a still-warm lantern from the table, lit it and threw on a coat. He would have no peace in his heart until he knew she had found a safe place to spend the night. Especially now when thoughts of the distraught Irish sailor haunted him from that first night; the one who had wandered away toward the ocean and was never heard from again. Just the thought of Olivia making some rash decision that could endanger her life sent his feet flying to the ocean for a quick look. *You couldn't have done something like that,* he thought in despair. *Not after all this. Not when I was ready to tell you how I feel about you. I don't care what the rumors are. I love you, Olivia. Love is strong enough to ride out any storm tossed our way. Please don't give up.*

A wind began blowing off the ocean, bringing with it the misty scent of brine and sea life, along with a dampness that chilled him to his bones. Olivia...out there somewhere, alone, without any covering or means of shelter. Alone, with no home and no hope. He wiped a hand across his brow. Why had he let this happen? Regret filled him. Regret for how he had acted toward her in the past. Regret for not having compassion and understanding for her losses and her plight. He of all people should know the pain of loss. Yes, he did save mankind as a surfman, but he also must think of the lost souls…the spiritually lost, like Olivia.

God, I need to have a true heart for the salvation of the lost. I'm sorry for being thoughtless. I'm sorry for not waiting on You and choosing Your path of mercy and understanding. I'm sorry for my selfishness.

With determination Jake headed for the streets of Hatteras, hoping beyond hope he would catch sight of her. The few people he found lingering on the street in the evening shadows only shook their heads when he inquired. At last he saw Georgiana walking swiftly by, her hands clasping a basket filled with goods for the house. "Georgiana!"

She paused, stared for a minute then shook her head.

"It's me. Jake Harris from the lifesaving station. Bodie's friend. I mean, Henry's."

"Oh, good evening. I was just heading back with these parcels."

"So I see. Please, do you have any idea where Olivia, that is, Miss Madison may have gone? I'm desperate to find her and make certain she's safe."

Georgiana shook her head. "No. I do know she was troubled with having no money and wanted to see the peddler tomorrow about her goods. But I don't know where she might have gone."

"All right. Thank you." Jake's heart sank. He felt no closer to finding her than he had been an hour ago. Reluctantly he retraced his steps back to the station. He knew the keeper would be angry if he was out past a certain hour, what with the board member arriving on the morn to begin the inspection. Right now though, nothing seemed to be going right. Despair tugged at his soul. In the darkness he heard the ocean roar. *God, please don't have her wander away in agony like that Irishman did the night of the shipwreck, lost in his confusion and pain. Please do not let that be Olivia's end.*

Exhausted, Jake stumbled onto the property of the station. Before entering, he glanced over at the storage building that housed the cargo. That cargo meant everything to Olivia. It also may have sealed her fate. He ought to check and make certain it was still secure. He didn't trust John not to place further evidence against Olivia's character.

When he arrived, he saw the door ajar and a slight movement in the shadows. "Who's in here? Speak!"

"J-Jake?"

Jake held the lantern higher to see a trembling figure wrapped in a ratty blanket. Dark eyes stared solemnly into his. "Olivia! Blessed be the Lord."

"I have nowhere else to go. Don't send me away."

He inhaled a deep breath, wanting to sweep the forlorn figure into his arms and hold her close. "Of course I won't send you away. But you can't stay in here. It's too cold."

"Just find me another blanket, and I will be fine. I have been in worse situations."

"You don't know how worried I was. I searched everywhere for you."

"How did you find me?"

"I heard about the situation from Sally. It was Bodie who asked that you leave the house. He was worried. I told him there was no reason, but he did what he felt he must. I'm truly sorry."

Olivia shook her head. "I don't know what to do or where to go. I have not heard from my uncle, either. I'm a stranger in a hostile land, accused by everyone and wanted by no one."

"That isn't true." He came inside and sat down beside her. "You're wanted by me. More than you know."

She didn't seem to hear his words. "How can you all believe I'm a pirate?" Her gaze lifted to meet his, her head shaking as if to mock the mere notion. "Just because I once carried a pistol and wear men's garments and I have cargo given by generous souls in England, it has branded me into someone I'm not."

"I don't know why this is happening, Olivia. But I'm glad you're safe. Truly I am." He gently enfolded her in his arms, pushing back strands of her limp hair that fell forward. His lips frantically searched hers, his heart wishing to protect her with every ounce of his being. When she responded with enthusiasm to his kiss, his love grew even stronger. "I won't let anything happen to you," he said softly. "I promise"

"Thank you. For everything. And for caring."

Her voice trembled with the last words. They kissed once more.

"I'll find you more blankets. And some food. I'm sure you're starving." When they parted, they stood and gazed at each other for a long moment. "Keep the lantern." He exited, closing the doors, sealing her from view...but not from his heart. Now an urgency rose within him, for Olivia's safety and for his own heart.

Until he came to an abrupt halt at the door of the station. A burly man, dressed in traveling clothes, was shaking hands with the keeper. Mr. Horner from the lifesaving board had arrived.

Chapter 12

Olivia remained huddled inside the shed, wondering what was taking Jake so long. She wished she had a better coat. One blanket with holes in it did not suffice against the raw and biting cold that seeped into her very bones.

She stood then, stretching her achy limbs, and began to pace. Every so often she peeked out the door. At first she thought she heard some commotion arising from the lifesaving station. Her heart beat furiously, imagining the men questioning Jake about the blanket and food. She knew how they all felt about her. Everyone in this place had branded her a criminal.

She paced until she came to a decision. She could no longer remain in Hatteras despite Jake's kiss and the words that spoke of his affection. She must seek shelter on the mainland and somehow make her way to her uncle's in Raleigh. She turned then to see the lantern cast a golden light over the wooden crates housing the precious cargo. If she did leave though, the cargo would be lost. It would mean turning her back on Nathan and committing him to a life worse than death. All the goods offered by friends and the lives sacrificed for the cause would be in vain.

Olivia peered once more at the station. *Jake, where are you?* The once proud Olivia Madison, the one who had cared for herself in England without asking for charity, now begged for someone to tend to her needs. How foreign it seemed. Until the words spoken by Mrs. Lears came to light. *You may not know why you are here. But God does. And He cares about that and about you.* Olivia had never really needed the workings of the Almighty in her life. Yes, she proudly spoke words of religion, as did most. It proved more a ritual than a statement of faith. She never truly believed there was some omnipotent being who had her best interests at heart. Now, forced by this predicament to find a place of refuge, without means or a future, with her brother's livelihood resting squarely in her hands, she had no choice but to trust and pray to an unseen God somewhere in the heavens.

God, I know I haven't prayed like I should. Or even devoted my life to Your care. But I do humbly plead with You now for help in this situation. Thank

You. She heaved a sigh, feeling at least grateful she could acknowledge the Almighty, especially with her strength lapsing. With that prayer came an unusual warmth and a feeling of heaviness in her eyelids. In those wee hours, sleep finally won her over.

Olivia was abruptly awakened at dawn to the sound of voices just outside the building. She rubbed her eyes, confused by it, when the door suddenly burst open. Golden sunlight poured into the darkness, revealing the face she had dearly wanted to see last evening. "Olivia, it's me."

"Jake! Where have you been?"

"You need to come with me."

At last he had found her a place to rest her weary head and warm her shivering body. Blessed be. God had indeed answered her prayer, and so quickly. She vowed then as she followed him back to the station to always pray, in every situation…

She stared at the contingent waiting for her arrival. From the grim expressions decorating every face, they were not in a cheerful mood. And standing among them was a man with a revolver—the town constable.

"Are you Olivia Madison?" the constable inquired.

"Yes. What is this all about?"

"On behalf of the lifesaving board, we are placing you under temporary restraint," directed a man with a quivering moustache, dressed in a fancy broadcloth coat and trousers. No doubt he was the official the station was expecting these many weeks. And somehow he had been made privy to the accusations heaped on her good name.

"I don't understand…" Olivia looked to Jake for support as the constable took her by the arm, ready to escort her away. "I've done nothing wrong."

The surfman Jake had called John began to chuckle. "You're not very clever. One of the pieces you planned to sell in town came right off the Dutch ship near Currituck. You would have done better to find a less conspicuous piece."

"That is enough," said the man with the moustache. "We will look into the matter further. The constable is in charge until the details can be sorted out."

Olivia threw another bewildered look toward Jake before being hurried away. He appeared oblivious to her condition. A wave of despair and betrayal coursed through her. *Jake...how could you do this to me? You kissed me. You said you would help me and never let anything happen to me.* She silently screamed at the betrayal. *I will never trust in a living soul again!*

Jake would never forget the look of horror that marred Olivia's beautiful face. He felt like Judas, bringing her out to the station, only to have her arrested by Mr. Horner and the constable. John had successfully won the argument linking a Delft plate

Olivia planned to sell to one that possibly came from a ship bearing Dutch markings and cited in the warning issued by the Currituck station. Between this coincidence and the letter warning of piracy off the waters by some woman captain, it proved enough for Mr. Horner to order her detained for further questioning. Jake felt as Olivia did in this place, without friends and without a future. Most of all, he had let another love slip through his fingers, all because of his work as a surfman. It began eating a hole in his heart that he feared would never heal.

Just then Grayson patted him on the back "Don't take this so hard, Jake. You did what was right in turning her over to the authorities. It's better this way. Ever since she came here, things haven't been right. You must have sensed it, too."

"She is not some beguiling woman, Grayson. She was shipwrecked, and she was in need."

"She is not who she appears to be. Sometimes our hearts, needy and hurting in their own right, blind us to the very things that can put a relationship on dangerous ground. We see what we want to see to satisfy our need. It's like love becomes a web, keeping us from knowledge. Which is why our Lord admonished us not to become entangled in the affairs of everyday life."

"So you're convinced she's a pirate because of a dish found in the room at Sally's home? And because the ship in question also happens to hail from Holland?"

"Only God knows the real truth. But we won't know until we question her. If she is blameless, God will be her defender. Not you or anyone else."

No! How could any of them do this to her? As if she hadn't been through enough, what with the shipwreck and her other losses. Not to mention her brother, who she'd risked everything to save.

Jake thought back then to his own life and the loss he'd endured. He would never forget his brother, Thomas, caught in that storm off the coast in their private fishing vessel. He'd been thrown off the boat in a violent tempest. Jake had tried desperately to grab hold of the young man's hand that waved frantically from the churning, gray waters. The scene remained forever branded in his mind, watching Thomas sink into the murky depths, never to be heard from again. Grief overwhelmed him, as did the pain of guilt from that day. After that, he vowed never to let another living soul drown.

Now Olivia was drowning in a sea of man's own making, from some farfetched idea contrived in a madman's mind. Like Thomas, she was reaching out to him, and he had ignored her cry for help.

But no more. He would save her, even if it cost him everything.

Jake left Grayson to seek out the perpetrator of this whole scheme. He found John working the lines, untangling what was needed before storing it back inside the shed. He glanced up then as Jake stared at him. "If you aren't doing anything, come help me get these lines ready before Mr. Horner does his final inspection."

At first Jake wanted to refuse the man. Instead he thought it a good plan to go ahead and oblige in the hopes John would reveal his true intent for ensnaring Olivia. He took a hunk of roping and began working out the knots.

"If you didn't realize it, I don't want the station to close on account of mismanagement," John started. "I will do anything needed to make sure we survive as a station." John gave a grunt and undid the snag. "Good, that looks better."

"Does that include having a young woman falsely accused?"

John halted in his work and reached over to grab a dipper of fresh water out of the rain barrel. "What's that supposed to mean?"

"You claim you would do anything. I'm only wondering why Olivia, that is, Miss Madison, is being used in this way. To what end?"

"I do not wish a deceiver and a pirate to get the best of the ships we serve and use this station to conceal stolen property. She fit the description. The plate in her possession was a piece of Delft pottery, from a ship that pirates attacked and…"

"You are quite far-reaching with your accusations to cast that kind of doubt on a woman's character. She's been through a shipwreck. Her crew died."

"Which is what they jolly well deserved with the thievery they committed on the high seas."

Jake dropped the rope. Tension gripped his muscles. "You have no real proof, and you know it."

"I hardly expect you to agree, seeing as you are involved. But I would be careful, Jake. Such loyalty could cost you your job." He picked up the roping. "I have several friends who would very much like the job working as a surfman. And I will advance in rank. It is already being talked about. Second sounds good to me."

Jake gritted his teeth but forced himself to remain calm. "You won't get away with it."

"I already have. She's in jail where she belongs. Just be sure you don't follow." With that John strode away, a whistle piercing the air. A sense of helplessness descended on Jake. He was no closer to an answer than when he'd arrived, and now he found his own place here at the station in jeopardy. The cost was growing ever greater, and the consequences ever graver as this situation continued in a downward spiral. It seemed like Thomas all over again…his hand reaching in vain for salvation from the deep…and Jake's inability to do anything on his behalf. *God, what am I going to do?*

Jake continued in his work though his mind was far from his duty. All he could think of was Olivia languishing in some strange place in Hatteras Village, awaiting the decision of Mr. Horton and the other officials. Most likely she would be taken to the mainland, perhaps even to Raleigh for questioning. He paused. *Raleigh.* The dwelling place of her uncle.

If only the uncle could be informed of this. He would lend his voice to this situation. He would tell them all that his niece was no pirate, that her intentions were honorable in rescuing her brother.

Then he considered the opposite course of events, that John's claims were true. Maybe she was not the woman he thought she was. What if there was no uncle as she claimed? The cargo had really been stolen from a helpless ship, and the Irishman who'd disappeared the night of the shipwreck had done so to avoid capture. If only there was some way to stem the flood of doubt and find out the truth.

After work that day, Jake stole away from the station in the hope of seeing Olivia. He had to know what he believed in his heart—that she was falsely accused of a terrible crime. If it was true, he would do everything he could to see her set free, even if it cost him his job. He would not allow the innocent to languish in some cell of judgment while he did nothing.

Jake arrived at Hatteras Village to search around town for some clue regarding Olivia's whereabouts. Finally he saw a few crusty fishermen talking with each other. He hailed them and they returned the greeting.

"Aren't you a surfman at the station?" asked a burly man who had just set down his nets.

"Yes, I am. We've been busy with the member of the board arriving for the seasonal inspection."

The man nodded as he elbowed his companion.

"We hears you've been pretty busy in other ways. That you all caught a pirate. It's all over the fishing fleet. Can't believe it myself. I thought those days were long past."

At this, Jake felt every hair stand on edge. "Well, that's what I've been told."

The man leaned over. "It weren't no man, neither. Did you know the pirate is some gal? Can you believe it? Caught her wearing men's clothes and with stolen goods. I never knew no thieving woman except for that Bonny long ago, and the piracy down in the isles." He folded his arms. "Something we don't need around here, that's for sure. Got no use for thieving liars. Sooner she's gone, the better."

"I would be interested to know exactly what she stole and from where. We've had many shipwrecked passengers looking for their possessions. The idea she may have interfered with one of those ships…"

"She got the goods off some Dutch ship up north."

"Any rumor as to what happened to the so-called pirate here in the village? We sure don't want to hear of someone like that escaping and returning to the station to cause trouble."

"I hears they got her down at some storehouse temporarily, near the south end. It's guarded, of course. Soon they're a'gonna take her to the mainland. But maybe you can talk to her. A lot of good that'll get you, though."

Jake thanked him for the information while engaging him in further small talk about the day's catch. Soon he wished them well and hurried off. Clouds rapidly covered the skies and hid the sun, as if nature mourned Olivia's misfortune. He cringed at the man's comparison of Olivia to some hated criminal of the past. Olivia Madison was no Anne Bonny, the notorious female pirate of the eighteenth century. He felt certain of it, more than he had before. All he could see before him was her large eyes staring at him, pleading for help. Jake swallowed hard. He had to help her. There was no choice as far as his emotions were concerned. This was a matter of life or death, as it always was here by the ocean. And life must win.

Olivia was thankful to have been brought to this place where at least she had been given a proper coat for warmth and several blankets. But the looks given by those who kept watch did little to ease her misgivings. Hopelessness ruled the day and the night. Everyone had abandoned her. Even Jake. *Especially* Jake.

She wiped a tear that escaped down her cheek. She'd thought at least Jake would stand by her side as he said he would. He possessed strong Christian virtues, or so she thought. Then the way he held her so tenderly and even kissed her. How could he do this to her and deliver her to her captors?

At times she tried to talk to the man guarding her, telling him she was innocent. The heartfelt plea received laughter in response. Now, more than ever, she understood the plight of Nathan in his predicament, day after day, without hope for the future. She had tried hard to free him, and now she found herself in a similar situation. All appeared lost.

Suddenly the door flew open. Daylight pierced the darkness. She saw two men walk in. Her legs nearly collapsed beneath her. One of the men was Jake!

"Thank you, sir," Jake said, handing him a coin. "I'm sure you will be given a commendation for keeping guard so well. Now if you would permit me to interview this prisoner in private so we can learn more about the piracy activities. Lives and cargo depend on what I find."

"Yes, indeed." The man nodded and left the room, shutting the door behind him.

"Are you all right?" Jake asked. "I was so worried."

"What concern is it of yours?" Olivia spat. "Thanks to you, I'm here in this miserable place."

They stared at each other for a moment or two, neither knowing what to say. Jake shifted his feet. He looked off into the distance as if trying to find the words. "It's not because of me. It's because of others who have it in their minds to do this for gain. I had no choice."

"How many times must I say that I'm no pirate? In your heart, you must know."

"Yes, I know. But no one else does. The surfman John has mounting evidence for it. They are convinced the pottery you planned to sell to the town tinker was from the Dutch ship in the northern shores near Currituck."

"A dear friend of the family donated it from England! Why, even my uncle has relatives that live in Holland!" Olivia shouted before Jake shook his head and held a finger to his lips, pointing to the guard just outside the door. She lowered her voice. "All of that cargo is for my brother. If my uncle were here, he would vouch for me a hundred times over."

"Why hasn't he come? What is his delay? It makes no sense he would not respond." Again he seemed to search for the words and the meaning behind them.

Olivia twisted her lips. "You don't even think I have such a relative, do you? I—I thought you were different, Jacob Harris. Out of all these men here, I thought you would believe. You who looks for the good in others by believing and trusting in them. But you're just like everyone else."

"Olivia, I want to help…but…"

"Then if there is any compassion left in you, find my uncle in Raleigh! Do this and you will know the truth."

Jake shook his head. "I can't leave the station on such a quest. I will forfeit my job and John wins." He winced when he said the words.

Olivia grew quiet. She could see he was in a difficult position, weighing her rescue here with the countless others out to sea. "Then send a telegram to my uncle for me. I will give you the details. And pray hard that it works, because there isn't much time left, for you or for me." She gave Jake the name and location of her uncle and her urgent telegram describing her predicament and asking him to come immediately.

"I hope he does come," Jake said softly. "I don't want to see you like this, Olivia. I've rescued too many to see you trapped in a cell with no way out." He drew closer. "Will you believe me when I say that despite all this, I do love you? You have a will to survive. You have done so against terrible odds and journeyed all the way here. I can't believe God would let you languish in some cell as your reward. I refuse to believe it."

Olivia stared at him and the seriousness of his words, illuminated by his eyes that gazed steadfastly into her own. For the first time in many long days, hope sprung anew. She was not alone. She had not lost Jake, as she'd feared. Perhaps God was looking out for her welfare after all, despite the bleakness of this situation. "I will believe you if you do everything you can to set me free so we can both work to free others."

"I will." Jake reached out to her, hoping that she would want to kiss him. She didn't see how, after his betrayal. But somehow, a strength that went beyond their own senses tugged their hearts into an embrace, and the kiss they shared in this barren place brought rays of hope to them both.

Chapter 13

"I can do nothing."

Jake stared, even as he twisted his felt cap in his hands. "Sir, you must. She has no other recourse."

"I can hardly involve myself in matters having to do with the board's decisions," said the keeper. "Obviously there is enough suspicion to hold her until further inquiry can be made."

He inhaled a deep breath. "Then may I have a leave of absence to fetch her uncle from Raleigh and resolve this?"

The keeper looked at him over the rims of his reading spectacles. "We are in the main season of work with the station. How can I let you go?" He paused. "Do you honestly believe she has an uncle in Raleigh?"

"Why wouldn't I?"

"It seems to be me this woman has not been forthright from the beginning. Women don't venture out on strange ships with men, seeking to deliver goods to these shores. They also don't sail the seas, plundering at will, then contrive clever stories to mask their true intent as this woman has done."

Jake could scarcely believe what he was hearing.

The keeper leaned across his desk. "I fear for you, young man. Already your actions of late speak of one who doesn't take the sincerity and honesty of this station to heart. I have seen my crew fractured by this. You and this woman always appear to be in the center of it. Now you want me to give you leave to find some fictitious uncle." The keeper shook his head. "If you wish to leave your post as a surfman, that is your decision. But you will not be welcomed back. That is all I will say on the matter."

Jake felt like an unseen fist had been driven into his stomach. He could barely breathe let alone move. When he finally found his feet and willed them to leave the office, he stood in the hall, stunned. Every door in his life had been sealed shut. Another soul would drown, and again, he could do nothing about it. Nothing for Olivia.

Jake walked numbly outside and headed toward the ocean. Many a life had been spared from those waters, thanks to his efforts. He had done his best with the lifesaving equipment and the skills he possessed. Maybe therein lay the resolution. Up to this point, he'd tried to do everything in his own strength. Wasn't God the one who gave the strength and will to do His good pleasure? He also gave such ability to help one's fellow man in times of need. In God's hands rested life and death. Jake could no more control it than the wind and the waves.

But Olivia's fearful eyes and quivering lips haunted him at every turn. How could he turn his back on her? He'd at least send off another message to this uncle, per her instructions. But what if the lack of response meant there was no uncle, as the keeper surmised? That beneath her reserved and feminine ways lay a woman he knew nothing about. Was she a woman who could cleverly disguise her intentions as easily as dressing in men's clothing and taking command of a ship? A woman who had swept him away with her fictitious tales and maybe love itself?

"I need to know, Lord," he prayed as he walked the beach, watching the waves lap at his feet. "I need to know what to do. Just like the lives out there on the ocean, my life is in Your hands. Tell me what to do."

Several days passed without a word from Jake or even news if he had sent the telegram to Olivia's uncle. During her detainment, one official inquired about the seafaring vessel she'd sailed from England. Olivia refused to answer the question. What did it matter? No one believed her anyway. No matter what she said, these men had all but proclaimed her guilty.

Even Jake stood on the throes of casting her to the wind. Despite his kiss of reassurance before he left, she worried he didn't believe her. She could see the indecision in his stark blue eyes and the way his gaze shifted, along with his stance. Without him, she had no one.

Suddenly the shadow of a woman appeared before the entryway, carrying a basket. When the figure entered the light, a familiar face and gray eyes looked at her.

"Mrs. Lears!" Olivia stood to her feet. She'd never expected to see a woman like her here. Maybe she came to stare or serve as a spy for Sally and the ladies of the sewing circle. Or to inform her that a pirate had no business infiltrating an innocent circle of friends.

"I could scarcely believe my ears when I heard the news," said Mrs. Lears, shaking her head. "I plan to speak to someone straightaway about this. It's shameful."

Hope burst forth in her heart. "Thank you. Have you…have you seen Jake at all? That is, the surfman, Mr. Harris?"

She shook her head. "No, I haven't. He and the others are very busy with the visitor from the lifesaving board. I did see them all out with the equipment earlier today." She drew up a chair and sat down. "I can't believe you're in this place," she repeated. "Whatever did you say that made them think you're a pirate?"

"It isn't what I said. It's that I exist. Now I am no better than my brother."

Mrs. Lears's eyebrow rose. "I don't understand."

"We are both imprisoned on false accusations. My only thought in coming here to America was to set him free by selling the goods I carried from England. Instead I've made everything worse."

"Never give up hope, my dear. I believe things will change soon. When situations are at their worst, it usually means things are ready to be at their best."

"I don't see how. But I hope you're right."

"I know I am. Life is always sending storms our way. As you know from the ocean, it's what we do in the midst of the storm that proves us. You need to weather this one right, and I know in the end, you'll be better for it." She stood to her feet. "I baked you some fresh muffins. Enjoy them and think of the friends that do still exist here in this world. Most importantly, don't lose heart. Or faith."

Olivia took the bread with thanks. When she bit into a delicious muffin bursting with berries, she thought of God. When hope had seemed lost, a friend had come her way, bringing with her bread to eat. The symbolism brought something else to mind. All at once she ran to the door. "Mrs. Lears!" she called.

The woman whirled. "My goodness!"

"Please…can you bring me one other thing? I—I have need of a Bible."

"Of course, my dear. I would be glad to bring you a Bible." She smiled, nodded and hastily left. Just saying those words, *I have need of a Bible*, gave

Olivia a sense of peace, though she didn't know why. Within the pages of that special book, she was certain to learn the answer.

Not long after, a Bible was delivered to the room, and she promptly opened its tattered edges. The book had seen fair use, but from within its pages fluttered a small note and verse. Psalm 46. Remembering, Olivia quickly sifted through the paper thin pages until she found the verse:

> God is our refuge and strength, a very present help in trouble.
>
> Therefore we will not fear, though the earth be removed, and though the mountains be carried into the midst of the sea…

The words leaped out from the pages and grabbed her soundly. Oh, how her heart yearned for words that spoke of strength in the midst of trial. But it taught her so much more—of the gale and wave that were overcome with His help. The storm that caused so many to meet their fate still tasted of His strength. He was with them, whether alive on this earth or embracing eternity in that final hour. His very presence was assured despite the circumstance. Olivia closed her eyes. She had no need to fear, though her fate still remained in question. She offered a prayer, not of hopelessness but thankfulness. Without this storm, she may have never come to know God's strength or His presence.

* * *

Jake could hardly concentrate on his tasks, despite having Bodie by his side. At times the young man would pause and stare at him, his lips parted as if wanting to say something. Then he'd returned to his duty in silence alongside Jake, coating the surfboat with wood tar to protect it from the sting of seawater. Mr. Horner had nearly completed his observations of the lifesaving activities, and soon they would hear his final judgment. The men were on edge, wondering if their station would suffer the ax as rumors circulated. Normally Jake would care also, but right now, all he could think about was Olivia. Despite the doubt that sometimes infected his thoughts, he truly believed in her innocence. She had come here in a desperate attempt to save her loved one and, in turn, had been caught up in a scheme that was not her doing. But the keeper refused to give him the leave that might exonerate her. John would not give up his claim, as ludicrous as it sounded. No one offered support but were caught up in the workings of the station. He felt as she did—that they were stuck like a ship cast on the shoals, splintered, unable to sail, awaiting a rescue they feared would never come.

"I haven't seen you this quiet since the day Rose left you," Bodie murmured.

Jake cast him a sharp glance, wishing he hadn't brought up such a disturbing subject. It only spoke of further failure in his life. Perhaps God never meant him to find happiness in a relationship. Maybe, like he'd once claimed, his lady would always be the sea. The surfmen once scoffed by calling Olivia his lady of the sea. But the real lady appeared a murky green ocean of whitecaps and nothing of flesh and blood. "There isn't much to talk about these days," he finally said.

Bodie heaved a sigh, resting the paintbrush back inside the bucket. "I miss the way things used to be, Jake. Going out on the beach patrol. Having good talks. Even with the rescues and the anxiety of it all, just working together to see people saved, we… we were like brothers. I never had a brother, you know. Just two older sisters. I miss talking to you about things."

Jake paused, the paintbrush in hand as he stared at the surfboat reflecting the rays of sunlight. A chill coursed through him at the idea of brothers. It seemed the common denominator in all the stories. Olivia's brother in the debtor's prison. His brother dying in the ocean where he now practiced lifesaving. And Bodie's yearning for a true brother. Might they not all be brothers by sharing in the good times as well as the bad? By caring for each other and looking out for one another?

Jake frowned and rested the paintbrush alongside Bodie's. "Sorry I wasn't there for you, Bodie."

"I—I knew you were angry that I asked Sally to send Olivia away. Now I wish I hadn't done it. I don't believe she's a pirate. It wasn't worth losing our friendship."

"Thanks for saying all this. I thought I was the only one who believed in her innocence."

"No, there are others. Grayson doesn't believe she's a pirate, either."

Jake straightened. "But what about all those things he said?"

"He wants to be the keeper one day, so he has to be careful and weigh all the facts at hand. But he told me privately he doesn't believe it. He's a lot like you, Jake. Very religious."

"We just believe in God, whose strength is greater than our own." *And I'm starting to recognize that more and more as time goes by.* He paused then, inhaling the salty sea air, when he saw two figures approaching the boathouse where they worked. One was a fine man sporting whitish whiskers and wearing a fashionable coat and top hat. The other was roughly dressed, with reddish hair and whiskers.

"Beg pardon," said the man with red hair. "Do ye work here?"

"Yes, we work here at the lifesaving station." Jake offered his hand. "I'm Jake Harris."

"Maybe you can help. I think I do recognize you. Yar the fair lad who saved my lass."

Jake blinked. "I don't understand."

"This is he," the man confirmed to the older gentleman wearing the coat and hat. "He brought her back in this strange contraption, safe and sound I might say. He thought nothing of his life that terrible night."

The man removed his hat. "Thank you for saving my niece's life, young man. Now we must find her. Do you know where she is?"

Jake could barely contain himself. "Did you say niece? Could you be..."

"Pardon me for not introducing myself. I'm Dwight Browning, uncle of Olivia Madison."

Bodie stared, his eyes looking as if they might tumble off his face. "I don't believe it," he whispered.

"And I'm O'Malley," announced the other man. "I don't know if you remember me. I was the one who was also rescued along with the lass."

"I... We...we thought you had drowned the night of the rescue!"

"No, far from it. Though my spirit was sore, and I did wander away. Abandoned my post, I did. Truly a cowardly act." He hesitated. "I couldn't face the lass after the shipwreck. But I thought after my days of mourning about what I could do to help. I remembered all she said of her uncle. I went seeking him, all the way to the fine city of Raleigh."

"This is amazing," Bodie repeated.

"And you are just in time, sir. Olivia has been jailed for piracy."

Mr. Browning's mouth fell open. "What on earth? Piracy!"

Jake quickly divulged the details and where she was being held.

"That is the most outlandish thing I have ever heard!" He jammed his hat back on his head. "You will take me at once to see this Mr. Horner. It's absolutely outrageous to imprison an innocent young woman, who is my niece, no less. Someone will pay for this."

Jake hurriedly led the men to the station and announced Mr. Browning and the crusty sailor to the keeper. Back outside, several of the surfmen gathered after hearing the commotion and the strangers entering the station. "Who are they?" John asked.

Bodie answered smugly, "They are Miss Madison's uncle and the sailor who served as first mate on board the ship. And if I were you, John, I'd get out of here quick before it's too late."

Olivia cradled the small Bible night and day, clinging to the words that brought strength. Worry and doubt tried daily to weaken her. She had seen the constable the day before, and he mentioned some kind of special proceeding on the mainland to hear the case and bring forth evidence. No doubt they would seize the rest of the cargo and use it for their bidding to fortify the false charges made against her.

She could sense then a bit of what Jesus went through, though His conviction led to his death. Yet life in jail might as well be a sentence of death, in her eyes. She was here to help Nathan overcome a pitiful existence and now found herself staring at a similar fate. "Oh, God, how could it have come to this? You know my innocence. I pray for an answer."

Just then she heard an array of voices. A man's

booming voice filled the air. She heard the jingle of keys and stood to her feet. They had come already to take her to the mainland where they would hear the evidence. Tears filled her eyes as she held the Bible close to her. She murmured another prayer. *God, my life is in Your hands. Whatever comes of this, I can do nothing but trust in You.*

Suddenly a craggy but familiar face filled the void of darkness as if a full moon had risen. "Why, my lass, you're lookin' a bit peaked, I must say."

It can't be. She blinked her eyes rapidly to make certain this was not some kind of dream. "O'Malley?" She could barely say his name.

"Yes, indeed. It's no vision you're seeing, lass. I didn't resurrect from the dead. Though the few days after the shipwreck were like death. My soul felt like it, too. So maybe I did." O'Malley nodded to the young jailer who had opened the door.

"I—I can't believe it." She fell out of the room that acted as her cell and into the man's outstretched arms. He had grown frail since their last meeting on the ship before it wrecked. "You crazy Irishman. Where have you been?"

"I have someone I'd like you to meet." He stepped aside to reveal an older man with a white beard, dressed in a frock coat and black trousers. He removed his silk top hat and bowed slightly.

Tears sprung into Olivia's eyes. She needed no introduction, though she had never met the man. She knew who he was. He had the kind but strong face of her mother. "Dear Uncle."

The man's eyebrows rose. "I can't believe you knew it was me. We have never met." He gladly offered her an embrace. "I'm happy to finally meet my sister's beloved daughter."

"My heart told me it was you. You came at last."

"I owe it to your first mate here. He sought me out."

"Didn't you receive my letter? Or the telegram I asked to have sent?"

Uncle Dwight shook his head. "No. And we have been traveling for many days, so a telegram may have missed us. But it doesn't matter now."

"But what of the accusation of piracy? Is the cargo still safe?"

"I have spoken to the men in authority. All is well. The gentleman from the lifesaving board offered his sincere apologies. The man who brought forth the false accusations is being punished. And the cargo is intact and being transferred to my care as we speak."

While Olivia should be overjoyed at this news and more than overjoyed to see both O'Malley and her uncle, a concern overshadowed it all. Where did Jake's heart rest in all this? What would become of him and their love?

Chapter 14

Winter was slow to leave the Outer Banks. The Christmas season had come and gone with little in the way of fanfare. Several of the men had gone to be with family for the day. Bodie had invited Jake to spend Christmas with Sally and her mother.

They had tried to make it a joyful time, but everywhere loomed the memories of Olivia. Like the day Jake met her after she found refuge in Sally's home. Then the encounters they'd had afterward, inside the shed and then in the warehouse when he'd kissed her.

He'd heard nothing from Olivia since she departed with her uncle that fateful day back in late October. He reflected on that day when she thanked him for all he had done to help her, accompanied by a quick kiss to his cheek. Before she left, she had pressed something into his hand.

Now he fished out the tiny gift from the pocket of his trousers and stared at it for the umpteenth time. It was a small knife she said belonged to her seafaring father. The knife had been in her pocket the night of the shipwreck. Imprinted on it was the family crest. He was grateful for this symbol, but his heart yearned for Olivia herself.

He considered taking time to venture to Raleigh and seek her out, but his sense of duty kept him here on the coast of North Carolina where the bone-chilling winds and fierce waves of nor'easters came and went. The tasks of lifesaving had begun in earnest as ships took to the cold waters. There was plenty to do over the next few weeks to mask his sadness of another love lost.

Jake entered the station outbuilding that day to see about some maintenance. Several of the surfmen had left for other jobs, including John, who took up a position north in Currituck. The keeper himself took a new position on the mainland. Grayson was now the temporary keeper and had begun training several new surfmen. It only seemed right in Jake's eyes that a godly man would run a lifesaving station. There wasn't a better way to illustrate the Bible, helping them do what they did best. Saving the lost.

"So what are you doing, Jake?"

He looked up to see his young friend Bodie. Since

the day Olivia had been exonerated from the accusation of piracy, Bodie had done all he could to rebuild the friendship damaged by the situation. Jake harbored no ill will for his friend and told Bodie that many times.

"I thought maybe I'd check out some of the equipment. We'll be using it quite a bit in the coming months."

"Which will be good for you, no doubt," Bodie said thoughtfully.

"And good for you, too, with the wedding coming."

Bodie's face turned bright red. He and Sally were set to wed come June after the main lifesaving season ended. Despite the activity of the station, Bodie took any spare time he had to forge plans with his love for the big day. They had found a small cottage to set up housekeeping. The final act was when Bodie asked Jake to stand in as his witness. Jake was more than honored. "I'll be glad when it's over," Bodie confessed. "Sally is doing so much planning, and I'm not allowed to visit while they are sewing the wedding dress. She says it's bad luck."

"Come help me look over the breeches buoy system and take your mind off the wedding plans."

Bodie obliged as they took down the heavy canvas to search for any weaknesses in the structure. Jake couldn't help remembering holding Olivia as they were dragged through the frigid ocean waters to safety. He reflected on their last kiss shared inside the storehouse during her imprisonment before her uncle and first mate had arrived to set her free.

He swallowed down his disappointment, wishing he could have been more involved in her freedom. He wished duty had not kept him from what he wanted to do on her behalf. No doubt by now she had found a suitable suitor among the rich men of Raleigh. Once more his love proved only the sea, as cold and unforgiving as ever.

"You're quiet all of the sudden. Are you thinking about Miss Madison?"

He shrugged.

"You ought to meet Sally's friend Priscilla. I think she would make a good match for you, Jake. If you want, I'll have Sally introduce her."

He shook his head. "No. No more. I've had two failures in love. I can't take a third."

"They're not failures. It's finding the right one. You just haven't yet."

Jake knew it was useless to talk about these kinds of things with a prospective groom. He knew how he felt and what he ought to do. While he'd made the decision that love was not in his best interest, his thoughts still remained on Olivia. Just before she and her uncle had left for Raleigh, Olivia had spoken to him for a brief time, thanking him for his help. She bestowed a swift kiss on the cheek as if they had only ever been acquaintances.

He wondered about that until his fingers touched the knife in his pocket, the knife Olivia had given him. He took it out then, examining the crest of the Madison family and pondering what it must mean to her. She'd endured much to see her family preserved, despite great odds. Even though she was no longer here, he was grateful for the time when their paths had crossed.

Suddenly Jake righted himself. What on earth was he doing, pining away here on these islands as if waiting for another ship to come in? Why didn't he do something about his feelings? His heart was beckoning for him to act. "Bodie, I…I need to leave."

Startled, the young man stared at him. "What? Where are you going?"

"I need to find my destiny once and for all. I'm going to Raleigh."

The young man's expression turned into a wide grin. "That's the best idea I've heard from you in a long while. Just be back soon. We're in the lifesaving season. We can't do this without you."

"I need to speak to Grayson and let him know."

"Let me know what?" announced an authoritative voice.

Jake whirled to see the older man, his mentor in many things in life, standing in the doorway to the boathouse. "Grayson, I need to go to Raleigh. But I will return."

"Praise be to God. I thought you'd never leave."

Jake stared, his mouth falling open.

"What I meant is, I knew all along you should seek out Miss Madison, but you had to discover it for yourself," Grayson said with a wink. "But I need you back here. I can send for a substitute for the weeks you'll be gone. But you must return within the month."

"I will." Jake smiled and hurried back to the station to fetch a few possessions for the trip. It would take time to get to Raleigh from the coast. A week at least. Maybe longer. He would travel as quickly as possible to see her beautiful face once again.

Olivia stood by her uncle's side, polite as always whenever he asked men to come dine. This day Uncle Dwight had invited to the noontime meal a wealthy gentleman with a curled moustache who kissed Olivia's hand when he arrived. Each time she stared at these visitors' faces as they consumed the meals and then watched out of the corner of her eye as their large hands sought to hold hers during an evening walk along the cold streets of Raleigh. Despite these encounters, her heart refused to entertain their interest.

Uncle had been firm that she needed to find someone who would meet her needs. The man must have a good rapport with people and be of good stature and wealth. Olivia would rather he were kindhearted, concerned and a man of godly character, yet she dared not contradict her uncle. He had her best interests at heart, after all. Many times he and the big Irishman would gather in the drawing room, imbibing spirits and talking at length. And she would roam the halls, thinking she could hear the ocean and reminisce on a time past.

On a few occasions Olivia did bring up Jake's name to her uncle's ears. While he respected the man in his position of saving lives, Uncle Dwight showed no other interest. No doubt he blamed Jake as he did all of them for the situation they had placed her in. But for Olivia, all was forgiven. Had it not been for Jake, she would not have survived the shipwreck nor would she possess the cargo which had been sold to pay for Nathan's release. Just a few days ago she had received the joyful news of Nathan's freedom. A close friend of her uncle's had traveled to England on business, carrying with him the money to free her brother. Nathan would accompany the man back to America on the next available ship. Best of all, for all its strange twists and turns and Jake's involvement leading to her false arrest, she'd discovered a face-to-face encounter with her savior Christ. She learned what it meant to have God as her refuge and strength. For that, she would be forever thankful.

"Now you must seek something worthwhile to do," Uncle Dwight told her as he observed her thoughtfulness. "There are sewing circles. A reading group."

Olivia smiled but politely declined. She recalled the sewing circle she had attended with Sally and how embarrassed she felt at not knowing a single stitch. Rather she preferred riding one of Uncle's prized stallions and wishing his home was closer to port so she could observe great ships coming to call. On the heels of this, he promised her a trip to Charleston one day.

"I'm going for a walk," Olivia informed the maid, who fetched her a cloak. "Please tell my uncle I shall be back for afternoon tea."

"As you wish, miss."

Olivia donned the cloak and headed out into the brisk February air. She missed the roar of the ocean. She never thought the sandy banks of the North Carolina coast would leave such an impression after the emotional turmoil of being branded a pirate. But in a strange way, the idea of one so brave and yet so devious intrigued her. Perhaps the thought titillated her adventuresome spirit, tempered by the regality of a lady. Still she would love to sail vessels to lands unknown, despite the danger. She wanted to live carefree, like the seagulls that frequented the beaches and squawked in an effort to obtain a morsel of bread. She wanted to touch the heavens, soaring far above the troubles life could bring. Most of all, she wanted peace to reign in her soul.

Olivia walked the street, her hands burrowed in a muff, greeting the few people that braved the cold. When she rounded a corner, she found a burly constable interrogating what appeared to be a disheveled beggar of a man, wearing a black fisherman's cap. She observed the exchange as the constable jerked the man's arm. She stepped back, wondering if it were some ruffian, until she peered closer at a crop of brown hair and a face that appeared oddly recognizable.

"But I seek the Browning residence," the man pleaded.

"You seek it to steal, no doubt. I know your kind. We've had many ruffians in the streets these days."

"I am no ruffian."

"Does Mr. Browning know you?"

"His niece does. Her name is Olivia Madison."

Olivia's hand flew to her mouth. Her heart suddenly began to race. *It couldn't be, could it?* Without even thinking she hurried forward. "Jake?"

He whirled. "Olivia!"

"I don't believe it!" She turned to the constable. "I am Dwight Browning's niece, and I will vouch for this man. I do indeed know him."

The constable frowned but reluctantly released Jake. He lifted his hat. "Sorry for the misunderstanding."

Olivia stared at Jake, who stood still and silent. He appeared unkempt, with matted hair, soiled clothing and a bearded face. He must have walked endless days to come here. How he'd ever managed the journey, she had no idea. And then to be labeled a ruffian and possible thief by the town constable. It suddenly made her laugh.

"What's so funny?" he asked.

"I was once labeled a thief. Now you. Are we destined to forever be misunderstood, Mr. Harris?"

Jake grinned. "I pray not." He hesitated. "I—I missed you."

"I missed you, too. Come to my uncle's home. You are most welcome."

"Am I?"

"Of course you are." The firm tone surprised even her, but she knew now, the moment she saw him, that he was her heart's desire. To be with Jake Harris, the saver of lives and souls, who made his home among the waves and the sands; there could be no other. She linked her arm through his ragged coat, though he tried to pull away, pointing to his disheveled clothing. "Really, I hardly care how you look," she admonished him. "It does not measure the man on the inside. But I will gladly do for you what you have done for others. Take care of you. Feed you. Give you a place to rest."

"Olivia…I…." He halted. "The reason I came all this way is to say…I can't live without you. I—I don't want to lose you. I know I've done things wrong. I wasn't there for you like I should have been during all those troubles. I made promises that I could not keep. I worried more about my job than you."

"Dearest Jake, you don't need to apologize. It has worked out for the good, as Scripture says. Besides, I would never want you to put my life above another's need for a rescue. I couldn't live with myself if that were the case."

He stepped back and stared. "I wasn't sure. Grayson and Bodie, they both said I should come here. That it was the right thing to do."

"They are right. It is." Tears drifted into her eyes. "You don't know how much this is an answer to prayer."

"Oh, Olivia." Jake didn't care about propriety or the way they looked just then in the streets of Raleigh. He took her in his arms and kissed her long. When they parted, she took his hand and led him to her uncle's home. "I have good news, too. Nathan will soon be joining us."

"Your brother? He's been released?"

"Yes. It has been a long hard journey, but we were able to get the money to him through a good friend of Uncle's. Nathan is out of prison now and, as soon as he is able, he will join me here."

"I'm so glad for you, Olivia. You have fought long and hard to see him set free. I do save souls from shipwrecks. But sometimes true freedom can take much more work and determination." He paused. "That's what drew me to you. I stayed at Hatteras during the past few months until it finally came to me to make the journey here. Only..." He paused. "They want me to return. It is the main lifesaving season. I want to be here with you yet I feel committed there also."

"Of course you need to be there. People need you."

He opened his mouth as if to say something else but promptly shut it when Olivia led him into her uncle's home. She escorted Jake to the drawing room, where her uncle sat, smoking a cigar. "You remember Jake Harris, Uncle."

He stood. "Of course. What brings you all the way here to Raleigh of all places?"

"Your niece, sir." He paused. "I haven't even asked Olivia this…but I want to marry her."

Both Uncle Dwight and Olivia stared at him in astonishment.

"I love her, sir," he continued. "I can provide for her with my job. My good friend is getting married in June. I would very much like to make it a double wedding, if you will permit us, sir. And if Olivia will agree."

"I—I don't know what to say to that, young man," Uncle Dwight began. "You both have been through a great deal." He hesitated. "However, I trust in my niece's judgment. Far be it for me to judge the matters of the heart. Especially as I have learned how much you did to help Olivia while she was there at Hatteras."

Olivia stood still and silent. Never had she expected Jake to travel all this way and with a proposal in hand. She thought then of all the suitors she'd had, from the lords of England to the men who had come to dine at her uncle's table. In all these, her heart had remained unclaimed. Until now.

"Yes," she said with a smile.

Jake grabbed her hand. "Yes? Olivia!"

"Yes." She accepted his embrace and another kiss until Uncle Dwight issued a loud "ahem."

"I think the young man could use some freshening up after his long journey. And some food."

Olivia laughed. "Yes, indeed. With all my heart." Her heart sang a song of thanksgiving for the lasting love of her rescuer who came upon the wind and the waves.

* * * * *